THE CASE OF

Counterfeit
Cash

THE
NICKI
HOLLAND
MYSTERIES
5

ANGELA ELWELL HUNT

Here's Life Publishers

First Printing, March 1992

Published by
HERE'S LIFE PUBLISHERS, INC.
P. O. Box 1576
San Bernardino, CA 92402

Cover illustration and interior artwork by Doron Ben-Ami
Cover design by David Marty Design

Library of Congress Cataloging-in-Publication Data
Hunt, Angela Elwell, 1957 –
    The case of the counterfeit cash / Angela Elwell Hunt.
        p.   cm. – (The Nicki Holland mysteries ; no. 4)
    Summary: Nicki is plunged into another mystery when she accidentally takes the
wrong suitcase from the airport and finds it filled with bundles of hundred dollar bills.
    ISBN 0-89840-339-1
    [1. Mystery and detective stories.] I. Title. II. Series : Hunt, Angela Elwell, 1957 –
Nicki Holland mysteries ; 4.
PZ7.H9115Car   1992
[Fic] – dc20   91-37700
                                                        CIP
                                                          AC

For Corey and Brooke

Laura

Kim

Nicki

Christine **Meredith**

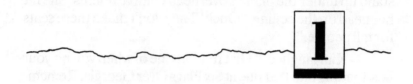

W e're almost home," Nicki Holland told her friend Kim Park. She looked out the airplane window as the jet gently lowered toward Tampa International Airport. "Want to look out the window?"

"No, I do not think so," Kim answered, squeezing her eyes tightly shut. "I just want my feet back on the ground."

Nicki laughed. "Honestly, Kim, you've flown before. Why are you so nervous?"

Kim opened one eye. "When we flew from Korea, I slept most of the flight. And when you and I flew to your grandmother's house last week, it was nice weather. But flying through that thunderstorm, with all those bumps — " She shut her eyes again and squeezed the armrests on her seat. "Are we almost there?"

The jet engines roared and Nicki felt the gentle thump of the plane as it touched down on the runway. "We're there," she said, reaching under her seat for her purse. "Home again."

"Good." Kim's dark eyes opened and she managed a weak smile. "But I will feel better when I am off this airplane."

Nicki shook her head. "I guess we should take a bus the next time we go to Atlanta."

"It was a nice visit," Kim said, unbuckling her seat belt. "And it was nice of your grandmother to invite me. Atlanta is a beautiful city."

7

"I liked Stone Mountain a lot," Nicki said, trying to stand up under the plane's overhead compartments. She hit her head on the ceiling. "Ouch! They don't make these seats for tall people."

Kim laughed. "That reminds me of when you hit your head getting into that ride at Six Flags Over Georgia. Remember?"

Nicki rubbed her sore head. "Yeah. Six Flags was the best part of the trip, even if I did bump my head. I only wish Meredith, Christine and Laura could have come, too. Maybe someday we can all take a trip together."

The crackle of the plane's intercom interrupted the girls. "Passengers should remain in their seats with their seat belts fastened until the plane has come to a full and complete stop," droned the flight attendant, and Nicki fell back into her seat even though everyone else was getting up. It was useless to stand up. They were packed onto the plane like Crayolas in a box, and no one could move until the doors were opened.

A flight attendant stood by the emergency door near Kim's seat. Kim caught her eye. "Are all flights as bumpy as this one?" Kim asked.

The flight attendant smiled. "Not all, of course," she said. "But Florida's famous for its thunderstorms. It's not at all unusual for us to ride through one on summer afternoons."

"Excuse me, miss?" A blonde lady in the seat across the aisle from Kim snapped her fingers at the flight attendant. "My dog is on this flight, too. Where will I find him? Are you sure he'll be okay? I worried about him the entire flight."

"I'm sure he's fine," the flight attendant answered smoothly. "Animals ride in a pressurized compartment."

"I wanted him up here with me, you know," the lady went on, snapping her chewing gum. "In fact, I insisted on it.

My little Sykes isn't used to being without me. He's a Chihuahua, you know, and he's really attached to me."

"Animals are not permitted in the passenger cabin," the flight attendant replied, but Nicki thought her smile seemed a little frayed. "FAA regulations."

"That's just not right," the lady huffed, pulling a stringy strand of hair out of her face. "Animals are people, too, you know."

"What on earth do you mean?" Two rows up, a heavy man with a bushy brown beard turned and shook his head. "I'd sooner fly with an ape than have a dog on the plane. I prefer to fly without the smell of dog assaulting my nostrils."

The blonde woman glared at the man. "Who asked you, fancy pants?" she snapped. "My dog makes better company than a snob like you."

"Madam," the man cleared his throat, "your pejorative comments meant to offend do not." He turned his back to the blonde woman and faced the front of the plane.

The blonde woman fumed. "I'll bet he's from New York," she muttered to the flight attendant. "Or some other rude place."

"Excuse me," the flight attendant sighed, stepping through the crowd. "I have to go to the back now."

The flight attendant squeezed her way toward the back of the plane and Nicki elbowed Kim. "I wish Meredith the Brain was here to translate everything that man said," she whispered. "Don't you?"

Kim didn't answer, so Nicki leaned forward to look at her friend. "Are you okay?" she asked, noticing that Kim's eyes were closed again. "We'll be out of here in five minutes."

"Just get me off this plane," Kim whispered. "I do not feel so good."

Kim looked better after they came down the ramp and into the gate area. Her cheeks flushed, and she smiled broadly when she spotted her parents standing with Nicki's family. She called a greeting to her parents in Korean, and Nicki waved to her little brother and sister.

"How was your trip?" Mrs. Holland asked, hugging her daughter. "Grandma took good care of you, didn't she?"

"The best," Nicki answered, giving her dad a quick hug. "And she told me to hug you two little guys, too." She hugged Sarah and reached for Joshua, but he squirmed out of her arms.

"Did you tell Grandma I'm six now?" Joshua spoke slowly, each word an effort. "I'll be going to kin-da-garden."

"She knows," Nicki said, winking at him. "And she said she's really glad you're going to speech classes, too."

"What about me?" Sarah demanded. "Did she send me a present?"

"Sarah," her mother scolded. "Don't be so greedy."

Nicki rolled her eyes. "Yeah, there's a present for each of you in my suitcase. But you have to wait until we get home. I'm not opening my suitcase in the middle of the airport."

"Nicki! Kim!" Nicki turned and saw Laura Cushman waving frantically from outside the gate.

"I didn't know Laura would miss us that much," Nicki said to Kim. "She didn't have to meet us at the airport."

"I do not think she is meeting us," Kim said, waving at Laura. "Look at her now."

Laura was no longer looking at Kim and Nicki. She squealed in excitement and waved at a very handsome young man who came off the ramp and caught Laura in a bear hug. He twirled her around, then put her down and hugged Laura's mother.

"Can we go see Laura for a minute, Mom?" Nicki asked, her eyes wide. "I've just got to know who that is."

"Sure, honey," her mother answered, laughing. "Give us a full report later. We'll meet you down at the baggage claim area."

Nicki and Kim ran toward Laura, who was hanging on to the arm of her mysterious guest. Whoever Laura's visitor was, he was clean-cut and about the most handsome man Nicki had ever seen. Dark hair, dark eyes, nice haircut, sharp suit . . .

"Nicki, this is my Uncle Kurt," Laura said, her eyes shining. "My mom's brother. Uncle Kurt, these are my friends, Nicki Holland and Kim Park."

Kurt stretched out his hand and gave Nicki and Kim a firm handshake. "Kurt Urban," he said, introducing himself. "It's nice to meet you ladies."

It was obvious that Mrs. Virginia Louise Cushman was delighted to see her brother. "You look great, Kurt," she said in her heavy southern accent. "And I couldn't believe you'd call and tell us you were comin' without letting us know when. So Laura and I played detective and decided just to meet you here. Weren't we clever?"

"Very clever." Kurt looked down at his sister and patted Laura on the head. "But I have some work to do before I can visit, so why don't I meet you at the house later? I don't want you to have to wait on me."

"Nonsense, Kurt. We'll just take you home now in the

limo and you can freshen up at the house. Your business can wait for at least an hour, can't it? Why, we wouldn't be hospitable if we didn't offer you a place to change and relax a little."

Mrs. Cushman rattled on, but Nicki noticed that Kurt Urban was no longer listening. He was smiling in her direction, but his eyes narrowed and followed the other passengers as they came off the plane ramp and milled about in the gate area. Suddenly he patted his sister's hand and cut her off: "Sorry, sis, but I simply have to go. I'll come to the house for dinner when I can, but don't hold anything for me. Laura, honey, you're more beautiful every time I see you. Now you go on home and I'll see you later."

He walked away with long strides and left the four ladies standing there.

"Why, I never," Mrs. Cushman shook her head. "Where have that boy's manners gone? I guess that's what living in a big city will do to a fellow."

"What city does he live in?" Nicki asked, trying to follow Kurt Urban's tall figure through the crowd.

"Washington, D. C.," Laura answered. "He does something with the government."

"Really?" Kim was impressed. "Is he a spy or something?"

Laura threw back her head and laughed. "Uncle Kurt a spy? Kimmie, spies are supposed to blend into a crowd. My Uncle Kurt could never do that. He's too handsome."

"For once, Laura, you're not exaggerating," Nicki said. She stood on tiptoe and spotted Laura's uncle in the middle of the crowd. He was leaning against a pole. Why? Was he meeting someone? Watching someone? Just resting?

"We had better go, Nicki," Kim said, tugging on Nicki's purse strap. "Our parents are waiting by the baggage carnival."

"That's baggage *carousel,*" Nicki corrected her. "Where the luggage goes in circles."

"I guess I'll see you two later," Laura said, looking a little disappointed. "Oh, I forgot to ask. Did you have a nice time in Atlanta? That's where I'm from, you know."

"We know," Nicki said. "And yes, we had a nice time with my grandmother. Maybe next time I can bring more than one friend."

"Only if we take a bus," Kim said, heading for the baggage claim area. "I do not want to fly again."

Nicki's father was waiting with Mr. and Mrs. Park in the baggage claim area.

"Where's mom and the kids?" Nicki asked.

"Joshua was climbing all over the baggage carousel," Mr. Holland answered. "She got tired of chasing him, so your Mom took Josh and Sarah to the car. Let's get your bag quickly. Joshua's been a real handful today."

Nicki understood. Many afternoons she had to babysit the two younger kiddos, and she knew how trying Joshua could be. The boy could wear out Hulk Hogan!

"We'll be lucky if the car's in one piece when we get there," she told her dad. "I'll grab my suitcase as soon as I see it."

"Which suitcase did you bring, Nick?" her dad asked, peering at the stream of suitcases spilling onto the carousel.

"The purple one."

"Great. That'll be easy to find."

Nicki laughed. The purple suitcase had belonged to her mother, but Nicki's father flatly refused to travel with it. "No self-respecting man would carry a lilac suitcase," he pronounced. So Nicki's parents had a new set of luggage, and Nicki used the lilac suitcase whenever she left home.

Nicki leaned back against a post and looked around. Kim was talking to her parents, jabbering away in Korean.

She was probably giving them a detailed description of her trip. The Parks hadn't been in the United States very long and they hadn't seen much of the country outside Pine Grove, Florida.

"J. T. Bence! Welcome to Florida!" Crabby Joe, a well-known restaurant owner in Pine Grove, was shaking hands with the bearded man from the plane. Crabby Joe's real name was Joe Wolfram, but somehow his nickname fit him better than his real name.

Even though Crabby Joe was enthusiastically greeting his guest, Mr. Bence didn't look very friendly. After shaking Crabby Joe's hand, he pointed out his suitcases and stood there stroking his beard while Crabby Joe gathered the luggage together and carried it out.

Brother, thought Nicki, *you'd think that guy was the King of England or something.*

The flight attendant from Nicki's trip passed through the crowd. She wasn't smiling now. In fact, her lips were pressed tightly together. Her steps were long and purposeful, and she pulled her small suitcase through the crowd without looking at anyone. In less than two minutes she had covered the inside of the terminal and was hailing a taxi at the sliding doors.

"Paging Marion Novak!" a steward called. He stood at the edge of the crowd with a cart.

"I'm Marion Novak!" The gum-chewing blonde woman pushed her way through the crowd. "Is that my baby? Sykes! How are you, honey?"

The steward reached into a small crate on the cart and brought out the most fragile-looking dog Nicki had ever seen. It was a Chihuahua, and he was shivering.

"Poor baby," the woman carried on. "Did they shut

you up in that horrible pen? Was it cold on that plane?" She looked at the steward without batting an eye and said, "If anything happens to this dog within the next week, I'll sue the pants off this airline, buddy."

The steward closed the door of the crate. "Hey, don't tell me, lady, tell the airline." He pushed the cart away, whistling.

The steward pushed the cart past a man Nicki recognized—Kurt Urban. He was alone and had a leather briefcase in his hand. He glanced at his watch, checked to see if he was at the baggage carousel unloading from Western American flight #2603, and patiently rocked back and forth on his heels. He looked like a tired business traveler ready for a good dinner and a place to relax.

Nicki was going to elbow Kim, but she was still talking to her parents. Nicki wondered if she should go over and say something to Mr. Urban. Would she be intruding? Was he really in town on business? What sort of business could anyone in Washington have in a tiny town like Pine Grove? Maybe his business was in Tampa, a big city.

"I see it," Nicki's dad interrupted her thoughts. "The purple suitcase. You stay here and I'll get it."

Her dad edged his way through the crowd toward the carousel and the lilac suitcase coming his way. He grabbed it and excused himself through the crowd until he was back at Nicki's side.

"Mr. and Mrs. Park, it was good to see you," he said, bowing his head in response to Mr. Park's gentle bow. "We'll see you again real soon. I've got to get Nicki home by five o'clock."

"What happens at five o'clock?" Nicki asked.

Her father didn't answer.

3

S urprise, Nicki!"

After Nicki's dad turned on the light switch in the front hall, Christine Kelshaw, Meredith Dixon and Scott Spence peered out at Nicki from the kitchen.

"Hey, you guys," she said, dropping her suitcase and purse in a pile by the door. "What a great surprise! I didn't expect to see you all so soon."

"Nicki, put this stuff in your bedroom so the rest of us can walk in the house," her mother grumbled, trying to come through the door. "I nearly broke my toe on your suitcase."

"I'll get it," Scott volunteered. He picked Nicki's suitcase up and made a face. "Purple? Where did you ever find a purple suitcase?"

"It was my mother's," Nicki said, pointing down the hall. "Just drop it in the first room on the left, Scott. Thanks."

"Your mom told us to order pizzas," Christine said. "They'll be here by five o'clock."

Mrs. Holland laughed. "Pizza sounds a lot better than me cooking for all of you. Now you kids get out of my way and I'll pour the Cokes."

Nicki and her friends went to the den. "We called Laura to come over, too," Meredith said, sitting in an easy chair. She swung her legs over the arm. "But no one answered the phone at her house all afternoon."

"She was at the airport," Nicki said, collapsing onto the couch. "Her uncle came in from Washington, D. C. He must have been on the same flight as me and Kim."

"I was hoping Kim would come home with you, too," Christine said, squirming in Joshua's small bean bag chair to get comfortable.

"She wasn't feeling very well," Nicki answered, smiling at the memory of Kim's scrunched-up eyelids. "We flew through a thunderstorm and she nearly got sick. And the plane we were on had a bunch of really strange people. I didn't think they'd ever let us off."

"Tell us about Laura's uncle," Meredith urged, leaning forward. "Is he anything like Miss Southern Belle?"

"Well, he's really good-looking," Nicki said, looking at Scott. "And nice. From what I can see, he's perfect."

"How old is he?" Christine asked, her eyes glowing with curiosity. "I've decided it's about time I found a boyfriend. I mean, Laura's always in love with somebody, Kim likes Jeremy Newkirk, and Nicki, you've got Scott — "

"Laura's uncle is too old for you," Nicki interrupted, embarrassed that Christine would mention Scott when he was sitting right next to her. "He's probably about twenty-eight. Maybe thirty. I don't know."

"I'll bet Laura's excited," Meredith said.

"I guess so," Nicki said, frowning. "The funny thing is, though, Kurt — that's his name — didn't seem to really want Laura and her mother at the airport. He said hi, hugged them and took off."

"Why would he do that?" Scott asked. "Wasn't he coming here to visit them?"

"I don't think so," Nicki answered. "He said he had business or something. He practically ran away from them, and later I saw him at the baggage claim area and he was just standing there, not in a hurry at all. It was weird."

"Well, you know Laura," Christine said, grinning mischievously. "Maybe weirdness runs in her family genes."

"Nicki!" Joshua ran into the den and tugged on Nicki's arm. "You promised you'd get my present from Grandma. It's in your tootcase."

"That's *suitcase*," Nicki corrected him. "You can open the suitcase and get it yourself. One of the presents is for Sarah."

"I alweady tried," Joshua said, still pulling on her arm. "The tootcase is wocked."

Nicki shook her head. "I didn't lock it. That suitcase is so old, I don't even have a key to lock it."

"It's wocked!"

Nicki sighed in exasperation. "You and Sarah bring the suitcase here. I'll open it for you and give you the present."

Joshua scampered off and Nicki rolled her eyes. "I know how you feel," Christine muttered. "I've got five brothers and sisters of my own."

"He's cute," Meredith said, dimpling. "I always wanted a little brother."

"No you don't," Nicki said, watching Joshua and Sarah push and pull her purple suitcase into the den. She got up to help them. "Sometimes you guys are more trouble than you're worth."

Nicki turned the suitcase on its side and tried to lift the latches. Nothing happened.

"That's strange," she said. "I know I didn't lock this. I *couldn't* lock it because I don't have a key."

"Maybe the lock is jammed," Christine offered. "The way they throw suitcases around at the airport, it wouldn't surprise me if the lock got busted or something."

Scott knelt on the floor next to Nicki and tried to lift the latches, without success. "Can you get me a screwdriver and a hammer?" Scott asked Nicki, peering intently at the suitcase latches. "I think I can spring these open, but I hope you don't mind if I hurt the suitcase a little."

"I don't mind a bit," Nicki said, turning to get the tools Scott needed.

Nicki found the screwdriver and a hammer in the garage and brought them to Scott. He and Meredith tinkered with the suitcase for a while, then Meredith frowned. "Something's not right here. Didn't you put a luggage tag on your suitcase?" she asked.

"Sure, I filled out one of those little paper tags when we flew out," Nicki said, looking at the destination tags still attached to the handle. "But it's not here anymore, so it must have fallen off."

"Maybe this isn't your suitcase." Meredith put a finger across her lips and her eyes grew wide. "It could belong to someone else."

"That's crazy," Scott snorted. "How many purple suitcases could there have been on that flight?"

Christine giggled. "How many purple suitcases could there be in the *world*? This is the only one I've ever seen."

"All the same, I think you should check your boarding

pass and see if the baggage claim numbers on your boarding pass match the tags on this suitcase," Meredith said.

"I threw all that stuff away at the airport," Nicki said, waving her hands. "I didn't think I'd need it."

"Then you should call the airport and see if any bags from your flight were unclaimed," Meredith said. "We'll keep working on the lock while you call."

Nicki and Christine went into the kitchen to call Western American Airlines. Nicki dialed the number and waited.

"Hello?" Nicki cleared her throat. "I arrived on a flight from Atlanta this afternoon, and I think I might have picked up the wrong bag. You see, I can't get my suitcase open, but I know I didn't lock it. So I was wondering if there was any unclaimed luggage."

Nicki listened for a moment. "There is? Is there an unclaimed purple suitcase?"

She listened a minute more, then clapped her hand over the phone. "He's going to check," she told Christine. "He said there are always unclaimed bags. How can someone forget to pick up their suitcase?"

A voice buzzed in Nicki's ear. "Yes, my name is Nicki Holland," Nick said into the phone. "You found it! I have the wrong bag? Oh, I'm sorry. We'll bring this one right back."

She hung up the phone and felt her face turning red. "I'm really embarrassed," she whispered. "Can you imagine? Two purple suitcases? And Scott's in there hammering on someone else's suitcase —"

"You'd better stop him," Christine said, punching Nicki in the arm. "He's about to destroy that suitcase."

In the second Nicki opened her mouth to call out a warning, she and Christine heard a loud *pop* from the den.

"We got it!" Meredith yelled.

"Oh no," Nicki whispered, "somebody's gonna be mad at us."

She and Christine rushed into the den and there on the floor was the open suitcase. But instead of the stranger's clothes they expected to see, the suitcase was stuffed with money — neat little bundles of money.

4

O hmigoodness!" Christine squealed.

"Quick, shut it!" Nicki snapped.

Scott slammed the suitcase shut and they stared at it as if it were a ticking bomb.

"Nicki," Meredith asked dryly, after the shock had passed. "What did you do in Atlanta—rob a bank?"

Nicki shook her head. "That's not my suitcase. My purple suitcase is still at the airport."

"Where did this money come from?" Christine whispered.

"It could be drug money," Scott said, raising an eyebrow. "Nicki, if you've got a drug dealer's money, you're in big trouble."

"Maybe it's some older couple's retirement money," Christine said, sitting on the floor. She tapped the suitcase thoughtfully. "They're moving to Florida and they don't trust banks."

"It really doesn't matter what the money is for," Meredith said, lifting the suitcase lid to peek inside. "What matters is that you have to take this back to the airport. You don't want this kind of responsibility, Nicki. It's too dangerous."

"But there's no tag or anything on the suitcase,"

Christine said. "What if nobody claims it? Doesn't Nicki get to keep it?"

Meredith shrugged. "If you lost a suitcase full of money, wouldn't you try to claim it?"

"Not if it was drug money," Scott pointed out, "especially if the feds were watching me. Or maybe the cops were tailing someone, and this money was to be used in an undercover operation . . . "

"You have a great imagination," Nicki said, still breathless. She lifted the lid of the suitcase and they gaped again at the stacks of bills. "How much money is in there, Meredith?"

Meredith started to lift a stack of bills.

"Don't touch it!" Scott warned her. "You don't want your fingerprints on drug money!"

Meredith made a face, but she pulled her hand back. "Nicki, do you have some gloves?" she asked.

Nicki thought for a moment. "My mom has rubber gloves in the kitchen," she said. "I'll be right back."

A couple of minutes later, Meredith slipped on the rubber gloves and lifted a stack of bills. She ruffled them. "This is a solid stack of one hundred dollar bills," she said simply. "This bundle alone is probably worth over ten thousand dollars."

"Here's a stack of twenties," Christine said, lifting them out.

"You're getting fingerprints all over them!" Nicki warned her, but Christine just shrugged.

"There's about a hundred twenties in this stack," she said, ruffling the bills. "That's what—two thousand dollars?"

"That's right," Scott said. He nodded as he counted

bundles in the suitcase. "There are twenty bundles in a row, and five rows of bundles," he said. "Half are bundles of one hundred dollar bills and half are twenties. How much is that all together, Meredith?"

Meredith closed her eyes to think. "That's fifty bundles of one hundreds and fifty bundles of twenties," she said. "That's five hundred thousand plus one hundred thousand — that's six hundred thousand." Her eyes opened wide. "Six hundred thousand dollars!"

"Wow! That's some nest egg!" Nicki said. "I hope it belongs to the old couple, and not drug dealers."

"Well, you'd better get it back to the airport," Meredith said, closing the lid. She peeled off the rubber gloves. "You can leave your name and address with the airline clerk. If no one claims the luggage within a month or so, maybe there's a chance you can keep it."

"What would you do with six hundred thousand dollars?" Christine asked. "Me, I'd buy a big house just for me and visit my family on weekends."

"I'd outfit a complete lab," Meredith said. "And discover a cure for cancer or something."

"I'd buy a red Ferrari," Scott said, laughing. "Make that seven Ferraris: red, black, blue, yellow, green, white and purple!"

"What would you do, Nicki?" Christine asked.

Nicki leaned back against the couch. "I'd pay for college, I guess," she said, "and buy some new clothes. I guess I'd tell Mom and Dad to put the rest in the bank or something, so I'd always have money when I needed it."

"That's our Nicki," Christine said. "Always practical."

"Not really," Nicki said. "I'm not going to have six hundred thousand dollars. Someone is looking for this money, and it doesn't belong to me."

Christine lay back on the rug. "Well, it was a nice thought while it lasted." Suddenly she sat upright, her eyes wide. "Hey! Maybe there's a reward! If you leave your name and address, maybe the real owner will be so grateful he'll give you a reward!"

"Someone told me you're supposed to give a reward of ten percent," Scott said, nodding. "That'd be sixty thousand dollars, Nick."

"That's *still* a fortune," Meredith said. "But I don't think drug dealers are going to give anyone a reward."

"Undercover cops wouldn't give a reward, either," Scott said glumly. "It's not their money to start with."

"Well, maybe we should just take a reward out while we have the money here," Christine said, shrugging. "Maybe a hundred dollar bill for each of us."

"No way!" Nicki protested. "That's stealing."

"Why?" Christine shrugged. "Four hundred dollars for reward money is a lot less than paying you sixty thousand."

"Forget it," Nicki said, snapping the latches on the suitcase. "I'm just going to tell my dad that we picked up the wrong suitcase and it needs to go back to the airport. I'll pick up my bag and leave this one behind. It's not my money and I don't care what happens to it."

"Nicki!" Joshua called from the kitchen. "Pizza's here!" He stuck his head into the den. "Did you get my present out of your tootcase?"

"No, Josh, I'm sorry. I brought home the wrong

suitcase," Nicki said smoothly, standing the suitcase upright. She led the way into the kitchen. "We'll ask Dad to take us back to the airport and get the right one."

"Awright," Joshua said.

Meredith and Scott followed Nicki into the kitchen, but Christine hung back in the den. "It really isn't fair," she muttered. "I mean, we really deserve *something* for being honest, don't we?"

She quickly unlatched the suitcase and slipped a twenty dollar bill from a bundle. She slid it into the pocket of her shorts and latched the suitcase again. "They'll thank me for this later," she whispered to herself.

5

"So the suitcase in the den isn't mine," Nicki explained to her father as they ate pizza. "My suitcase is still at the airport. Can you drive us over there to make the switch?"

Nicki's father grumbled, but she knew he wouldn't mind. "That's at least a half hour's drive," he mumbled, "so if you're all going, better hurry up and finish eating. I'd like to get back home before it gets dark."

"Can we all go?" Christine asked. "I don't want to miss this."

"Sure," Nicki said, flashing a warning at Christine. Her look clearly said, *Don't tell.*

"I'll be with you in a moment," Nicki's dad said, getting up from the kitchen table. "Just give me a couple of minutes to get ready."

"Can I go, too?" Joshua asked. "I want to get my present out of your tootcase."

"Suitcase," Nicki corrected him automatically. "And no, Josh, I think you had better wait here with Mom and Sarah. It'll be a long drive, and I don't want you to be bored."

The four young people went back to the den. Nicki frowned at the suitcase. "Is there any way we can lock it again?" she asked.

Scott nodded. "I think I can turn the locking

28

mechanism with the screwdriver," he said. "In any case, I don't think anyone can tell that we opened it."

"Except for this tear," Meredith said, pointing to a rip in the suitcase fabric near the latch. "But maybe they'll think it was just damaged in handling."

"If someone's getting six hundred thousand dollars, they can buy a new suitcase," Christine grumbled. "And Nicki, why didn't you want me to tell your dad about the money?"

Nicki shrugged. "I don't know. It's just a feeling. I wish we'd never opened this dumb suitcase, and the fewer people who know about it, the better."

"There!" Scott jiggled the latches on the suitcase and, as before, they didn't budge. "It's locked again. Or jammed again. Whatever."

"Good." Nicki breathed a sigh of relief. "I'll feel better once this is at the airport and I have my own stuff back."

Nicki assured her father that it would only take a minute to make the suitcase switch, so he let her and her friends out at the baggage claim area and waited in the car. "Don't take too long," he cautioned her. "If I'm parked here for more than ten minutes I'll get a ticket."

"We'll be quick," Nicki promised. She led the way, Scott carried the suitcase, and Christine and Meredith followed them into the airport.

Nicki went straight to the Western American desk. "I'm here to return a piece of luggage and pick up my suitcase," she said, smiling at the teenage boy behind the desk. "My name is Nicki Holland."

"Oh yeah," the boy smiled at her. "I talked to you on the phone."

Nicki felt herself blushing. He was young, probably only seventeen or eighteen, and looked really sharp in his uniform. She was sure that Christine and Meredith were drooling. "That's me," she said brightly. "Can I get my suitcase?"

"Sure." The boy smiled and his eyes scrunched up — was that a wink? Then he disappeared behind the partition. Nicki wondered what Scott was thinking. Was he jealous? He and Nicki were special friends, but that didn't mean she couldn't *talk* to another cute guy, did it?

"Here's your bag." The boy swung it out from behind the counter and placed it beside the suitcase Nicki brought. He laughed. "I don't believe it. Two purple suitcases?"

"I didn't believe it, either," Nicki said. As the boy placed the other suitcase behind the counter, Nicki asked, "By the way, did anyone else call? About the other purple suitcase, I mean."

"Yeah. Some lady did call, but she said she'd come by later. Oh yeah," he reached for a piece of paper, "she asked for your name and address so she could thank you."

"I knew it," Christine said, smiling at the boy. "It was an older lady, right? And I'll bet she was so happy to get her —"

Nicki kicked Christine in the shin and Christine abruptly shut her mouth.

"She was happy to get her suitcase back," Meredith said, finishing the thought.

Nicki reached for the piece of paper, but Scott grabbed her hand. "Nicki," he whispered in her ear, "what if it's drug money? What if they want to know who you are because you know about the money? It's dangerous to leave your name and address."

Nicki slid the blank paper back toward the boy. "It's okay," she said, her mouth suddenly dry. "She doesn't need to thank me. I'm only doing what anyone else would do."

"If you don't leave your name and number, you won't get the money if no one claims it," Christine hissed.

"Someone's already claimed it," Meredith muttered back to Christine. "The lady called, dumbo. She's coming to get her suitcase."

The boy watched Nicki and her friends whisper to each other, then he cleared his throat. "Is that all?" he asked, smiling warmly at Nicki. "Anything else I can do, Nicki Holland?"

He remembered her name! Nicki felt a warm glow rise from her toes. A really fine older guy had remembered her name!

"Nothing," she answered, smiling back at him. She picked up her suitcase. "I guess we're all done here."

"Okay." The boy smiled again. "My name's Dylan Ward. Call if you need anything else."

"Okay." Nicki turned around to leave, but Christine lingered at the counter.

"We live in Pine Grove, Dylan Ward," she said, her green eyes sparkling. "It's nice to meet you. I'm Christine Kelshaw."

Dylan grinned at Christine, and Meredith grabbed Christine's sleeve and pulled her away. "Come on, Chris," Meredith urged. "It's going to be a long drive home."

"Don't you just love a man in uniform?" Christine sighed as they left the ticket counter.

Scott gallantly offered to carry the suitcase, and Nicki looked around the airport as they walked out. The late afternoon crowd had thinned, but a few people still loitered in the chairs, on the telephones and in the wide halls.

"Hey," she said, stopping in mid-stride. "That's Kurt Urban! Over there in the chair. That's Laura's uncle!"

"Where?" Christine asked, squinting to look down the wide hall.

Just then a motorized cart beeped behind them, and Nicki and her friends had to step aside to let him pass. When Nicki could step back into the hall again, the man in the chair was gone. "I'm sure that was him," she said, looking around. "But why would he still be at the airport? He should have been at Laura's for dinner an hour ago."

"Maybe he's waiting on his luggage," Scott said, shrugging. "Sometimes you have to wait until the next flight before your luggage comes in."

Christine giggled. "Maybe he's waiting on his suitcase full of money," she said. "After all, Laura's rich, and this is her uncle, right?"

Nicki tilted her head. It wasn't such a crazy idea, except for two things. First, Kurt Urban didn't seem at all the type to carry a purple suitcase. Second, he seemed sensible. Surely no sensible person would carry six hundred thousand dollars for a short trip to Pine Grove.

"You probably just thought you saw him," Meredith said, not even looking up. "After all, you only met the guy for five minutes. Now you're seeing him everywhere."

Nicki kept walking and didn't answer. Maybe Meredith was right. Maybe she was just a little too overcome by meeting the handsome Kurt Urban and Dylan Ward in the same day. What was wrong with her?

"A good looking guy smiles at me and my brain turns to mush," she muttered to herself. "I should probably go through life wearing a blindfold."

6

Nicki was quiet on the ride home. Meredith and Scott were involved in an animated discussion on whether chimpanzees or dogs were better pets, and Christine was up in the front seat telling Mr. Holland all about how cute Dylan Ward was.

Something was bothering Nicki. Why had Kurt Urban been at the airport? Did the suitcase full of money belong to him? Why was he here in Florida anyway? He was young and single — maybe he was a little on the wild side, too. Could he be a drug runner? Could he be a spy?

A sudden idea struck her, and she leaned forward and hugged the back of the front seat. "Hey, Dad, would you mind taking us to Laura's? It's still early. I'd like to see her."

"Yeah, let's go to Laura's," Meredith chimed in. "We've got to tell her about Nicki's suitcase. She'll love that story."

"Are you sure she won't mind?" Mr. Holland asked, looking at Nicki in his rearview mirror. "Some people wouldn't appreciate four kids dropping in on them unannounced."

"If the Cushmans are busy, we'll come home," Nicki promised.

"What about the rest of you?" Mr. Holland asked. "Christine? Scott? Meredith? Is it okay with your folks if I take you to the Cushman's?"

"Sure," they all answered. Nicki was a little embarrassed. Honestly, sometimes her dad treated her like a little kid. Even though she and her friends had been solving mysteries for several months now, Mr. and Mrs. Holland always wanted to know where Nicki was and what she was doing.

When they reached the city limits of Pine Grove, Mr. Holland turned off the main road and headed out to Gatscomb Hills where Laura and her mother lived in a mini-mansion. Nicki settled back into her seat and sighed. Was she really curious about what could be a new mystery or did she just want to get another look at Kurt Urban? She wasn't sure herself.

"Why, hi, everybody!" Laura said, opening the door. She was wearing a short little robe over her bathing suit. "Come on in! You're just in time to swim with us."

"I don't know about that," Christine said, laughing. "We don't have our bathing suits."

"That's no trouble at all," Laura said. "I have bathing suits you can borrow." Laura looked at Scott. "Sorry, Scott, but we don't really have any guy's bathing suits."

"That's okay," Scott said, looking a little awkward. "I'll just take off my shirt and swim in my shorts, if that's okay."

"That'd be fine."

Mrs. Cushman came into the foyer, trailed as always by the sweet scent of her gardenia perfume. "Why, Nicki and friends," she said, smiling at them, "what a delightful surprise. Are you going to join us out by the pool?"

"Yes, Mother, they are," Laura said, closing the door. "Just as soon as I get bathing suits for the girls."

"We're sorry we didn't come prepared," Nicki said, trying to explain. "But we were out at the airport and just decided to come on the spur of the moment."

"Don't you worry about it," Mrs. Cushman said. "Y'all are welcome here any time. Go on, now, and get changed. In this heat the only place to be is in the water. Come on, Scott, and I'll introduce you to Laura's uncle."

Laura led the way up the stairs while the girls followed. "How long has your uncle been here, Laura?" Nicki asked. "Did he make it in time for supper?"

"No," Laura answered. "He just got here a few minutes ago. He was working, you see, and missed dinner. But Mom saved him a plate, so he's eating out by the pool." Laura looked at Nicki quizzically. "Now why are you so concerned about whether my uncle eats his dinner?"

"I'm not concerned about his dinner," Nicki said, leaning against the wall of Laura's bedroom. Laura opened her closet and pulled out several beautiful bathing suits on hangers.

"Nicki thought she saw your uncle at the airport," Christine said. "And can I have that green one? It's beautiful!"

"Sure. I thought it would look good on you," Laura said, tossing the green suit to Christine. "What about you, Meredith? How about this red one?"

Meredith looked at the red bathing suit a little skeptically. "I'm not sure I can fill it out," she said. "Why don't you let me have the black one."

Laura shrugged and handed Meredith a black bathing

suit. "Okay, Nicki, there's a red one, a flowered one and this one with polka dots. Which do you want?"

Nicki pointed to the flowered one. "Good," Laura said, tossing it to her. She sat on the bed as the girls changed. "Why do you think my uncle was at the airport? His flight came in at three-thirty, so why would he be there hours later? And what were you guys doing there this late?"

"Nicki took the wrong suitcase," Christine said, adjusting her straps. She looked in the mirror. "You're right, Laura, this is a cute suit. Anyway," she turned to Laura, "that's not the most exciting thing. When Nicki got the suitcase home, we opened it. It was stuffed with over six hundred thousand dollars!"

Laura's jaw dropped. "You're kidding."

"No," Nicki said, shaking her head. She folded her clothes neatly and put them on Laura's bed. "My dad picked up the wrong suitcase by mistake. So we locked the suitcase again and took it back to the airport, where my suitcase was waiting."

"That's where we met Dylan Ward," Christine added. "Honest to goodness, Laura, he was *fine.*"

Laura grinned. "Really? Tell me more."

Christine babbled on about how good looking Dylan was, and Nicki caught Meredith rolling her eyes. Nicki grinned, then picked up Christine's clothes from a pile on the floor. *Let them call me a neat freak,* Nicki thought, *I don't care.* A twenty dollar bill was sticking out of the pocket of Christine's shorts.

"What's this?" Nicki said, holding up the twenty dollars. "Christine, were you planning to buy the pizza or something?"

Christine broke off her conversation with Laura and her face reddened. "Uh, yeah," she said, coming over and taking the money from Nicki. She picked up her shorts and stuffed the bill back into her pocket. "What were you doing, Nicki, going through my stuff?"

"No," Nicki said, stepping back. She was hurt that Christine would even think such a thing. To cover her feelings, Nicki picked up a towel from Laura's bathroom and headed for the door. "I'm going swimming, if anyone wants to join me."

"We're coming," Laura said, gathering towels for the other girls. "And I want to hear all about this suitcase deal and especially about this Dylan Ward!"

Mrs. Cushman and Kurt Urban were in the spa at the end of the pool, and Kurt nodded politely when he saw the girls.

"Good to see you," he called to Nicki. "And it's nice to meet you other young ladies. I've already met Scott, and I believe he's waiting for you all in the pool."

Scott was sitting on a bench in the pool, and Nicki and her friends slipped into the water to join him. The pool was warm, almost like bath water, but it still felt good after a long, hot day. Nicki wished her family had a pool, too. It would be heavenly to jump in after working in the yard and getting all sweaty.

They splashed and paddled around for a few minutes, then Laura climbed onto a floating raft and paddled over to where Nicki was leaning against the side of the pool. "Now tell me about the suitcase full of money," Laura said, her eyes serious. "Is this a new mystery for us? Goodness, we haven't done anything since March when we helped Jeremy New-kirk."

"And that's when Kim got her boyfriend," Christine interrupted, thinking of their last mystery, *The Case of the Terrified Track Star*.

"I don't think it's a mystery at all," Meredith said, wading over. "Nicki got the wrong suitcase, returned it and now she has her own stuff. Case closed."

"But what was all that money about?" Scott asked. He pulled himself out of the pool and sat on the edge, dripping down on the girls. "Was it drug money? If drug dealers know that Nicki knows about their money, they could come after her, you know."

"It's not drug dealers," Christine said impatiently. "Dylan said it was some woman who called and asked about the suitcase."

"You don't think women can be drug dealers?" asked Meredith. "Drug dealing is an equal opportunity crime."

"I wonder if I should have called the police," Nicki said, rubbing her hands together. Funny, but the water suddenly seemed cold. A chill passed through her.

"I think you did the right thing," Scott said. "But I'd be careful if I were you."

"I still think you should have left your name and address," Christine said. "Imagine if nobody claims all that cash — the things you could do with six hundred thousand dollars!"

Kurt Urban had walked up behind Nicki unnoticed, and she was startled when his deep voice asked, "What's this about six hundred thousand dollars? Are you guys planning a major crime or something?"

There was a chuckle in his voice, but as he slipped into the water Nicki thought his eyes looked serious.

"Brrr," he said, then he swam past her with an expert butterfly stroke. He reached the far end of the pool, turned back, and swam to the group of young people. "I know this water is warm, but it seems cold when you've been sitting in the spa."

He pulled himself out of the pool and sat next to Scott. "So what's this all about? Who's the rich one?"

"Nobody's rich now," Christine pouted. She pointed at Nicki. "Nicki here decided to be honest."

"What are you talking about, nobody's rich?" Meredith mumbled. "You've got twenty dollars in your pocket. That's rich enough."

Christine defended herself, "That's really none of your business."

"I think it was drug dealers' money," Scott told Kurt earnestly. "And when the guy at the airport asked Nicki to leave her name and address, I told her not to. Was that a good idea?"

Kurt nodded, but his thoughts seemed far away. "Sounds good to me. Did you find out anything else about this suitcase?"

"Nothing really," Nicki said. "There was nothing in it but money. No luggage tags, nothing."

"When did you return it to the airport?" Kurt asked.

"I don't know, about forty-five minutes ago, I guess," Nicki said. Her brows rushed together. "Why?"

Kurt shrugged, but he stood up. "My, Virginia, that felt great," he called to Mrs. Cushman. "But I've got an appointment in a few minutes, so I'll head out now and see you later tonight, okay?"

He gave his sister a kiss on the cheek as she sputtered in confusion. "In and out again, in and out," she scolded him. "Why can't you be a proper guest and stay put?"

Kurt flung a towel around his neck and grinned wickedly. "It's just not in my nature, I guess," he said, and he walked into the house.

Nicki opened her eyes the next morning and yawned. A summer Saturday! Nothing to do but sleep and eat and read and call her friends — oops! She sat up. Today she had promised to go with Christine to Crabby Joe's. Christine had some big secret she wanted to tell the other girls, and she wanted to do it in Crabby Joe's ice cream parlor.

Nicki got up and pulled on a pair of shorts and a tee shirt. She knew she couldn't mention Crabby Joe's around the house because it was Joshua's favorite place. Crabby Joe bought his insurance from Mr. Holland, so Nicki's family often ate in the restaurant or stopped for ice cream in the ice cream parlor.

Crabby Joe's Fine Eating Establishment was located down on the waterfront, along the intracoastal waterway. The waterway was the western border of Pine Grove, and if you wanted fresh seafood, a refreshing dip in salt water, or a boat or jet ski ride, the waterway was where you'd go. A couple of miles down from Crabby Joe's, the intracoastal waterway spilled out into the Gulf of Mexico.

Whenever the Hollands went to Crabby Joe's, Nicki would take Josh and Sarah out to the picnic tables. They'd sit, slurp ice cream cones and watch the activity on the waterfront. Crabby Joe's restaurant sat on a skinny strip of beach, and Crabby Joe let anyone swim there who wanted to. On the right side of Crabby Joe's was a marina where about forty boats were tied to long docks. To the left of Crabby Joe's was a tiny post office that could be approached by land or sea, a small police station, and Landry's Bait and Tackle Shop.

But the best part of a trip to the waterfront was seeing Coal Island. In a small cove off the waterway, straight out from Crabby Joe's, thousands of pelicans nested on Coal Island. Nicki's dad explained once that Coal Island was a bird sanctuary, and the birds knew it was a safe place. Often pelicans covered the trees so thickly that the island seemed to move and cry like one big bird. In the spring and early summer, fuzzy baby pelicans peered out at passersby from their treetop nests, and always, no matter what season, the smell of bird droppings kept curious boaters at arm's length.

"It really stinks," Nicki told Joshua once, as she pointed across the water to Coal Island, "but if we ever get a boat, I'll take you over there to have a look."

"Dat's okay," Joshua had replied. "I'll just take a clothespin for my nose."

So today Nicki had to be sure not to mention Crabby Joe's or Coal Island. She and her friends would never get anything done if she had Joshua in tow.

As promised, Mr. Peterson, Laura's chauffeur, picked Nicki up in the Cushman's Rolls Royce limousine. Laura, Kim and Meredith were already in the car. Mrs. Cushman always gave the girls permission to use the limo, apparently feeling that if Mr. Peterson were along, they'd be safe and well-accounted for.

"What's this all about, Nicki?" Laura asked as Nicki got into the huge back seat. "What's Christine up to?"

"I have no idea," Nicki answered. She greeted Mr.

Peterson, then turned back to her friends. "Who can ever guess what Christine's up to?"

Kim was looking better today, Nicki noticed, and she seemed glad to be home and with her friends. "I heard about the excitement yesterday," Kim told Nicki, her eyes gleaming. "You were rich for half an hour!"

"Something like that," Nicki grinned. "But I'm glad it's over."

Mr. Peterson pulled into Christine's driveway. "You can honk the horn, Mr. Peterson," Meredith said. "Christine won't mind."

Mr. Peterson gave the horn a gentle tap, and Christine rushed out, carrying one tennis shoe under her arm and a hairbrush in her hand. "Hi, you guys!" she called, hopping into the car. She slammed the door and propped up her foot to slip on her other shoe. "Sorry, I was running late. Torrie, Gaylyn and I had to clean our room and it was more of a mess than usual."

She leaned toward the front seat. "Mr. Peterson, we're headed for Crabby Joe's, please," she told him.

"What is this all about?" Laura asked. "What are you up to, Chris?"

"Well," Christine looked at each face around her. She was about to burst with some overwhelming secret. "Two things. First, I thought we'd all enjoy doing something special today. I mean, it's summer and we're out of school, and we've really done some neat things for people this year. So don't we deserve something special?"

Nicki raised an eyebrow. "Like what?" she asked.

"We're going to rent a rowboat and go out to Coal Island," Christine announced. "It'll be fun, and I've got the money to do it. I think I even have enough for ice cream afterwards."

"That's really nice, Christine," Meredith said, impressed. "But are you spending all your babysitting money on us? Is that really what you want to do?"

"Actually, this is Nicki's treat," Christine said. She looked over at Nicki quickly. "Now, I know you didn't want to do this, so I didn't say anything earlier. But I figured you deserved a reward for turning all that money in. So when you guys weren't looking, I slipped a twenty dollar bill out of that suitcase. I didn't take it for me, honest. I planned all along to do something for all of us. I just thought we deserved it."

Nicki didn't have an answer. Taking money out of the suitcase was wrong, but what could she do about it now? She couldn't return it because she didn't even know who the suitcase belonged to. Maybe Christine was right. Anyway, what difference would twenty dollars make out of six hundred thousand?

Nicki sighed, aware that the others were watching her. "Okay," she said, throwing her hands into the air. "I just hope you guys know how to row a boat."

"What is your other news, Chris?" Meredith asked. "You said there were two things."

Christine bit her lip and looked at the girls. "It's the best part," she said. "Remember Dylan Ward? I called him!"

"You didn't!"

Christine nodded happily. "Yep. I called him at work, and he gave me his home number, so I called him later at home. We talked for an hour."

"Who is Dylan Ward?" Kim asked, a blank look on her face. "Did I miss something?"

"Only the best guy in the world," Christine said, closing her eyes. She threw her arms out and hugged herself. "I think I'm in love."

Oh brother, thought Nicki.

Mr. Peterson parked in Crabby Joe's lot and the girls raced down toward the marina's boat dock. A whiskered, wrinkled man was napping under the shade of an umbrella, and Christine loudly cleared her throat.

"I'm not asleep," the man grunted, his eyes still closed. "Just restin' my eyes. What do you want?"

"We'd like to rent a boat for about an hour," Christine said. She pointed to a big, beautiful sailboat tied up at the first dock. "Like maybe that one?"

The man's eyes flew open, and he peered suspiciously at the girls. "Not my *Puddleduck*," he said flatly. "If I give you anything, it'll be a calm quiet rowboat. Can you all swim? Do ya know how to row a boat?"

When they nodded, he grunted and pointed to a small rowboat tied up at the end of the dock. "Wear a life jacket, all of ya," he ordered. "Stay out of the channel or the bigger boats will run ya over. Don't set foot on Coal Island, and I'll need the ten dollars in advance."

Christine took the folded twenty dollar bill out of her pocket and gave it to the man, who carefully unfolded and pocketed it. He pulled a thin leather wallet out of his other pocket and gave Christine a ten dollar bill in change.

"Be back here at twelve o'clock sharp," he gave one final command. "And if ya drowns, it's not my fault. Got that?"

"We got it," Meredith said, leading the way down the dock.

It was a wide rowboat, so Nicki and Meredith sat on the back seat, Christine and Laura took the front seat, and Kim perched nervously on an upturned bucket in the middle of the boat. Meredith pulled five soggy life jackets off the dock and tossed them inside the boat before unhitching the boat from the dock.

"Do I have to wear this thing?" Laura said, holding her mildewed life jacket up with two fingers. "It's disgusting."

"Just keep it near you," Nicki said, "so you can grab it if you need it."

Christine gave the dock a big shove so the boat drifted away from the dock and into the current of the waterway.

"Wait," Meredith cautioned, holding up her hand. "Let this big boat go by before we start rowing."

A huge yacht motored slowly through the waterway, and its wake caused the little rowboat to bob up and down. Laura squealed.

Nicki grabbed the edge of the boat to steady herself and looked back toward the safety of the dock. A familiar figure stood there, a man shading his eyes and looking across the water. Was it Kurt Urban — again? It looked like him.

She started to say something to the other girls, but then she stopped. They already thought she saw Kurt Urban everywhere and besides, in the glare of the midday sun she wasn't sure who the man on the dock was. Better to forget it.

"I knew this would be fun," Christine said, putting her oar into the water. "Now let's go have a look at Coal Island."

"It's a rookery," Meredith explained, as they neared the island. Rowing was easier when they were out of the main channel and into the waters of the tiny cove. "This rookery is a colony of pelicans."

"Oh, the smell is too much!" Laura said, pinching her nose. "Smells like ammonia, only worse."

"Ignore the smell," Nicki told her. "Just watch the birds."

There was something fascinating about so many pelicans on one tiny island. Several of the birds, upset by the approach of the girls, left their nests and were hopping about from tree to tree.

"They are trying to take our attention from the nests," Kim said. "They are protecting their babies."

Several big pelicans took to flight, flying over the girls' heads in an effort to draw them away. "Don't worry," Nicki said softly. "We're not going to bother you."

As the girls rounded a corner, Laura gasped. There, hanging directly over their heads, seemingly in midair, was a dead pelican. "The poor thing," Christine moaned.

"Fisherman don't realize sometimes that the stuff they throw into the water can kill pelicans and other birds," Meredith explained. "This bird got caught in fishing line, flew here and then got caught in the tree. That's really sad."

The girls rowed under the tree with the dead bird and left it behind them. "We're on the back side of the island now, aren't we?" Laura asked. "I can't see Crabby Joe's anymore."

"Yeah, this is the back side," Meredith said. "It's quieter over here, isn't it?"

"It'd be a nice place for swimming," Nicki noticed, looking at the shallow beach along the cove. "We could swim here instead of at the beach at Crabby Joe's. Over here we wouldn't have to watch out for boats."

"That would be fun!" Christine said. "We could rent a boat, park over there on the shore and swim. Our own private lagoon."

"If we can stand the smell," Laura added, still holding her nose. "It's horrible."

"What's that boat ahead?" Christine said, pointing in front of them. "It looks like it's anchored here."

"Why would anyone anchor in this stinky place?" Laura moaned, trying to row with one hand and hold her nose with the other.

"The boat looks deserted," Meredith said. "Let's paddle around it and see if anyone comes out."

It had been a pretty sailboat in its day, Nicki thought. It was white, with a wooden strip down the sides and a tall mast which reached past the trees on Coal Island. But there were no sails on the boat, and a net which ran around the edge of the deck was tattered and torn. There were no signs of life, either on the deck or through the tiny portholes in the cabin.

"The *Mary Celeste II*," Meredith said, reading the name of the boat. "That sounds familiar."

"It's giving me the creeps," Laura whispered. "First a dead bird, now a dead boat. Come on, let's get out of here."

"Okay," Nicki agreed. They rowed quickly and skirted the edge of the island. Soon they were back out in the open waterway.

"Whew, I'm glad we're out of there," Christine said, turning around to grin at Kim, Nicki and Meredith. "Now that we can breathe again, how about some ice cream?"

8

The girls stood in front of Crabby Joe's ice cream counter.

"I'll have a double scoop of chocolate chip and butter pecan on a sugar cone," Meredith stated calmly. "With chocolate sprinkles on top, please."

Kim smiled at the clerk. "The same for me, too."

"Not me," Laura sighed. "I have to count my calories this summer. I'll have lowfat frozen yogurt — peanut butter flavor, please."

Nicki laughed. "I'd like mint chocolate chip in a milkshake," she said. "The chocolate chips all fall to the bottom of the cup, but I'll have one anyway," she told the girl behind the counter.

"I'll have a banana split," Christine said. "Loaded with everything. And extra napkins."

Christine paid for the ice cream with the rest of the money and the girls sat at a table under a slow-spinning ceiling fan. "This is a great lunch, isn't it?" Christine said, laughing. "Look how nutritious it is! Milk products, fruits, nuts —"

"And chocolate," Meredith said, pointing her spoon down at the chocolate sprinkles on her cone. "Chocolate is one of the four basic food groups, isn't it?"

"Sure," Christine said, licking her spoon. "Breakfast, lunch, dinner and chocolate desserts!"

"My mother would die if she saw me eating this for lunch," Laura said, taking a big bite of her yogurt. "But after rowing in the hot sun, this feels wonderful."

Nicki took another sip of her mint chocolate chip milkshake and looked around the restaurant. They were the only people in the ice cream parlor, but through the open doorway she could see quite a crowd in the restaurant.

Suddenly the grizzled man from the boat dock flew through the doorway with Crabby Joe behind him, his features contorted in anger. Behind Crabby Joe calmly walked the bearded man Nicki had seen with Crabby Joe at the airport. What was he doing here?

The men seemed not to notice the girls. "I tell you I'm not trying to cheat you," the boat man said. "I didn't know it was funny money. I just got it this morning." The man threw his hands up in exasperation, and as he did, he looked over and saw Nicki and her friends at the table. His eyes widened and he pointed at the girls. "From them! I got the twenty dollars from them!"

Nicki closed her eyes and hoped the men would go away, but when she opened them again, the man and Crabby Joe stood right at their table.

"Nicki Holland," Crabby Joe said, recognizing her, "Wiley says here that you girls gave him twenty dollars this morning. Is that true?"

Nicki threw a frightened glance at Christine, then she nodded. "Yes, we did," she said. "Is something wrong?"

Crabby Joe grunted. "Well, Wiley here has just eaten twenty dollars worth of lobster and tried to pay for it with a phony twenty dollar bill. I guess it's my job to find out if that money came from you girls."

Christine was as white as the vanilla ice cream in her

dish; her freckles stood out like purple blotches. Meredith was wearing her this-can't-be-happening look, and Kim looked sick again. Only Laura seemed unaffected.

"That's crazy," Laura said, wiping her mouth primly with her napkin. "We don't know anything about phony money. We are honest people, and we wouldn't cheat Mr. Wiley."

Wiley glared at Laura. "You're lyin', too, girlie," he said, shaking his finger in Laura's face. "I got that money straight from you girls, and I haven't gotten money from anyone else this morning. It was your twenty!"

Laura opened her mouth to protest again, but Nicki kicked her under the table. Laura didn't think the money was phony because she hadn't thought about where the money came from. But Nicki had seen the suitcase, with rows and rows of crisp one hundred and twenty dollar bills.

"Can I see the money?" Nicki asked. "The twenty we paid with was," she glanced over at Christine, "nearly new and crisp. I think it had only been folded once or twice."

Crabby Joe grunted and motioned for the gentleman from the airport, who produced the bill from his enormous hand. He tossed the bill onto the table, and they all stared at it.

"It looks real to me," Christine squeaked. "How do they know it's not real?"

"It's counterfeit," the man from the airport said. "My name is J. T. Bence, and I'm a New York restauranteur. I've learned to spot counterfeit cash in my business."

"But how do you know for sure?" Meredith asked, gingerly feeling a corner of the bill.

"Easy," Mr. Bence replied. He pulled a pen out of his

pocket and proudly held it up. "This is a counterfeit bill detector. If I run this over the face of the bill, it should glow with a green light because the amount of the bill should be printed in magnetized ink. As you can see here, this is not magnetized ink." Mr. Bence ran the pen-like device over the bill, and the light at the end of the device glowed red, not green.

"Wait a minute," Meredith said, digging in her pocket. She pulled out a one dollar bill. "Show me what that does on real money."

Mr. Bence sighed, but he ran the device over the words "one dollar" printed on the face of the bill. A green light on the device glowed.

"Real money also has ink that is not magnetized," Mr. Bence continued. "The Federal Reserve seal on the back of the bill is not magnetized. It should glow red." He ran his device over the back of both bills, and both times his pen glowed red.

Mr. Bence held up the fake twenty. "This is from an excellent counterfeiter," he said, "but they aren't using magnetized ink. And you have a problem here that the authorities should deal with."

"Are you going to call the police?" Christine asked, her voice squeaking. "It's my fault. I took the money out of the suitcase, so maybe I should go to jail. But I'm not a counterfeiter."

Crabby Joe looked down at the girls, then he nodded to Mr. Bence. "Why don't you let me handle this," he said. "Wait for me in the restaurant."

Mr. Bence walked away, shaking his head, and Crabby Joe turned to the girls. "The way I figure it," he said slowly, "is that you girls owe Wiley here a new twenty dollar bill.

And Wiley, you owe me twenty dollars. I don't want to send a group of girls or a fellow fisherman to jail, so I'll just call the police and hand this bill in. If you all will make it right, then we won't have to send anyone here to jail."

"I tell you what," a familiar voice interrupted. Nicki turned around to see Kurt Urban stand up. He had been sitting behind a screen of ferns and the girls hadn't seen him. *For how long?* Nicki wondered.

"I'm Kurt Urban, Laura's uncle," he said, shaking Crabby Joe's hand. "Let me pay both you and Mr. Wiley twenty dollars and we'll call it even."

"That'd be fine with me," Crabby Joe said, putting his hand out for the money.

"Good." Kurt smiled, giving Crabby Joe and Wiley each twenty dollars. "And since we're done with this deal, would you mind giving me that counterfeit note? I'd kind of like to keep it as a souvenir."

Crabby Joe's brow furrowed in thought. "Don't you know it's a crime to even carry one of these around?" he asked in a low voice. "Of course, I don't want to be mindin' your business, but it seems to me the police ought to know about this."

"The police have enough on their minds," Kurt answered smoothly. He opened his wallet again and handed Joe another twenty dollars. "There. I've paid for it three times. Now can I have it as a souvenir?"

"Why not?" Crabby Joe handed the fake bill to Kurt and he placed it carefully in his wallet.

"Thanks," Kurt smiled. "Now girls, since your ice cream has melted, are you ready to go? Mr. Peterson is waiting outside."

Nicki and the others piled into the Cushman's limo, but Kurt Urban was no longer anywhere in sight. "How does he do that?" Nicki wondered aloud. "He appears and disappears. And how did he end up at Crabby Joe's today?"

"I can answer that, Nicki," Mr. Peterson called from the front seat. "I happened to look through the window to check on you girls, and I saw that fisherman and Mr. Wolfram approaching your table. I figured there might be trouble, so I called Mrs. Cushman on the car phone. She must have sent Mr. Urban immediately."

"I'm so glad she did," Christine said, breathing a sigh of relief. "I just knew I was going to jail. Honestly, I never dreamed that money was fake. Do you think the entire suitcase was full of counterfeit money?"

"It had to be," Nicki said. "That's why it was in a suitcase in the first place. That's why the woman who called about the suitcase wouldn't leave her name at the claim desk. It's against the law even to possess counterfeit money."

"Then why did Uncle Kurt want to keep that bill?" Laura asked, her eyes wide. "I don't want him to get in trouble. What if he forgets it's counterfeit and accidentally spends it somewhere?"

"Maybe he really wanted it as a souvenir," Christine said.

"It was an expensive souvenir," Kim pointed out. "He spent sixty dollars in there."

"It seemed like he didn't want the police to get the counterfeit note," Meredith said thoughtfully. "It was almost like he would have paid *anything* to keep it from the police."

"Why?" Laura asked. "He's not a counterfeiter, if that's what you're thinking."

"We're not saying he is," Nicki answered smoothly. "But people might think he was. After all, he's the new guy in town." Nicki's mind began to work and her jaw dropped. Meredith caught her eye and seemed to read her mind.

Could it be? Laura didn't want to admit it, but Nicki knew it was very possible that Kurt was a counterfeiter. He was at the airport when the mysterious suitcase of money arrived. He was there waiting for something when Nicki brought the counterfeit money back. And when he heard Nicki say she had returned the suitcase full of money, he left the Cushman's house and went somewhere in a hurry. Did he know Christine had one of the fake notes? Why was he willing to spend sixty dollars to keep the police from getting a counterfeit bill?

Nicki closed her eyes and remembered how Kurt had carefully placed the bill in his wallet. He didn't do anything to keep his fingerprints off the bill. Was it because he really wanted it as a souvenir? Or were his prints already on six hundred thousand dollars of counterfeit money?

9

I was out at Crabby Joe's today delivering an insurance form," Mr. Holland announced at dinner, "and he told me the wildest story. Seems someone tried to pass a counterfeit note in his restaurant."

"Really?" Mrs. Holland asked, passing Nicki the lima beans. Nicki pretended to dole a spoonful on her plate, hoping her mother wouldn't notice. Nicki hated lima beans with a passion.

No use. "Nicki, at least try some beans," her mother said in an exasperated tone. "You, too, Josh. Why can't you two be like Sarah? She likes anything green."

Sarah grinned mischievously at Nicki and popped an extra-large spoonful of lima beans into her mouth. Nicki closed her eyes. Gross. She had always thought lima beans tasted like bits of mush with skin around them.

"What did Crabby Joe do?" Mrs. Holland asked. "What did the police say?"

Mr. Holland scratched his head. "You know, now that you mention it, Joe didn't say anything about the police. He just said that they caught the bill and everything worked out okay. He's got some guy visiting from New York, and if he hadn't been there, Joe says he would never have caught the phony bill."

"What's somebody from New York doing down here

in Pine Grove?" Nicki asked, stirring her macaroni and cheese.

Mr. Holland nodded his head and took a minute to chew a bite of his roast beef. "You won't believe it," he said, pausing to wipe his mouth, "but Joe is thinking about starting another restaurant in New York. Apparently he and this New York guy will be business partners."

"Mr. Bence?" Nicki asked.

Her dad looked surprised. "Yeah, that's right. How do you know him?"

"Um, he was on the airplane with Kim and me. Plus, we had ice cream today at Crabby Joe's and we saw the guy there."

Nicki hoped her dad's next question wouldn't be if she was there when the counterfeit money was passed, but apparently he never considered the possibility.

"Well, Mr. Bence seems nice enough," Mr. Holland said, "but a little distant. The entire time I talked to him he was looking over my shoulder. I guess insurance bores him."

"That could be," Mrs. Holland teased her husband.

Nicki decided to change the subject: "Um, a bunch of us are going to meet Monday at the beach next to Crabby Joe's. Is that okay?"

"Who's going to be there?" Mrs. Holland asked.

"Meredith, Kim, Christine, Laura, Scott and me," Nicki answered. "And Mr. Peterson. He said he'd drive us."

Mrs. Holland smiled. "I'd be glad for you to go, honey, but there's one problem."

Nicki's heart sank. "What?"

"I've got to take some clients house hunting for most

of the afternoon and your dad will be working, too. Do you mind taking Josh and Sarah with you? I'm sure they won't be any trouble. They love the beach."

Josh and Sarah cheered and clapped their hands even before Nicki said she'd do it. They knew she didn't have a choice. If she wanted to go to the beach with her friends, she'd have to babysit, too. "Okay," she sighed. "I'll do it."

They packed the limo with picnic baskets, towels, inflatable rafts and bottles of sunscreen. Whenever Mr. Peterson stopped to pick up someone else, squeals poured out of the doors.

"This is crowded, but it's fun," Laura said, balancing Sarah on one knee and Josh on the other.

"I just hope Christine doesn't have to babysit, too," Meredith pointed out, her long legs drawn up under her chin to make room for Kim, who was sitting in front of her on a picnic basket. Scott was riding in front with Mr. Peterson.

Mr. Peterson pulled up in front of Christine's house and gently tapped the horn. The door opened and a girl ran out. At first Nicki thought it was Torrie, Christine's older sister.

But it was Christine. Her hair was upswept in a new hairdo, and on her feet were backless sandals with tiny little heels. She was wearing a delicate lace coverup over her bathing suit. On her arm she carried a straw beach bag with a two-liter bottle of Pepsi sticking out.

"What happened to Christine?" Laura asked, giggling. "She looks like a Barbie doll!"

Christine opened the door and awkwardly stepped into the tiny space the others had left for her. "Hi," she said, looking down at the floor. Then she lifted her head and her green eyes were defiant. "Okay! I know I look a little different, but just leave me alone!"

"Why?" Nicki asked, trying to think of a reason for Christine's getup. "Did Torrie give you a makeover or something?"

"No," Christine said, pulling a mirror out of her beach bag. She checked her makeup and with a stubby finger she wiped away a smudge of excess lipstick. She looked away from the mirror and back at her friends. "If you must know, I called Dylan Ward and invited him to the beach with us. He's meeting us there. And I told him I was sixteen and I will not forgive any of you if you tell him I'm thirteen."

"You what?" Meredith shrieked. "You're going into the eighth grade, girl. You're not sixteen."

"He won't know any different unless one of you tells him."

"Why did you have to lie to him?" Kim asked quietly. "You are not sixteen."

"Well," Christine sighed, "I just didn't think he'd come if he knew I was only in middle school. And honestly, I'm not trying to marry him or anything. My parents wouldn't even let me date him. But I want a boyfriend, someone to hang around. I mean, Nicki, you've got Scott —"

"Scott isn't really my boyfriend," Nicki said softly, so he wouldn't hear. "We're just good friends."

"Well, you know what I mean," Christine said, putting her nose in the air. She turned to look out the window. "Dylan's coming. So don't any of you say anything."

Nicki, Laura, Kim and Meredith only looked at each other. Maybe Christine's little game wouldn't get her into trouble, but lately Christine and trouble had been going steady.

They arrived at the beach and carried their towels and baskets down to the waterfront. Mr. Peterson stayed at the car, but he pulled out a lawn chair, a beach umbrella and a long novel.

"I asked him if he wanted to come swimming," Laura told Nicki as they carried a heavy picnic basket down to the water, "but he said he likes to watch from a distance."

Josh and Sarah were playing tag with the waves. Nicki looked over at the marina where the bottom abruptly dropped off and the boat docks began. It was not safe to swim in boater's waters, and she'd have to remind Joshua and Sarah to stay away from the docks.

They all swam for a while — except Christine, who didn't want to get her makeup wet — then plopped down on the sand to eat sandwiches and drink cold Cokes from the cooler. A shadow fell across them, and Nicki looked up. There was Dylan Ward, just as Christine said he would be. Christine blushed, then invited him to join them.

"This is wild," he said, looking at their group. "Don't tell me the kiddies and the old geezer up in the parking lot are with you guys."

"He's not an old geezer," Meredith interrupted. "He's Mr. Peterson. He's our friend."

Dylan shook his head, and Nicki didn't think he seemed nearly as nice out here as he did at the airport. Away from work he was rude, and Nicki began to worry about Christine.

Christine sprang to her feet. "Come on, Dylan, let's

walk up to Crabby Joe's," she said. "We'll let these guys clean up. What took you so long? I've been waiting for you for an hour."

They walked off toward the restaurant, and Nicki smiled at Laura. "Laura, if you'll take Josh and Sarah down to the water, the rest of us will clean up this mess."

Laura brightened at the idea. "Why, I'd love it," she said. "You guys don't know how lucky you are to have little kids around. I'll go teach them to build sand castles."

Laura took Josh and Sarah by the hand and led them down to the water. Nicki began to pick up trash.

"I had to get rid of Laura because I don't think she's going to like what I have to say," she said quietly. Meredith, Kim and Scott listened carefully. "It looks like we're going to have to find the counterfeiters. It's really a job for the police, but Kurt Urban wouldn't let the police have the evidence they need, so Crabby Joe didn't call them."

"Joe probably thinks it's a one-time thing," Meredith said. "But we know it's not."

"We saw the suitcase full of money," Scott added. "And from what you've told me about yesterday, I'd bet the entire six hundred thousand dollars is counterfeit."

"If Christine had not taken out the twenty dollar bill, we would not have known that," Kim pointed out, handing Nicki a bag of trash. "So why is there not more counterfeit money being spent around town?"

"I don't know," Nicki said, stopping to think. "But if you had that much fake money, you wouldn't want to spend it all in one place. People would get suspicious. You'd have to spread it around."

"Like a traveling salesman," Meredith said. "Like

Kurt Urban, who travels a lot for his 'business,' whatever that is."

"He is the most logical suspect," Nicki said, brushing sand off her hands. She sat down on a beach blanket. "But what about that Mr. Bence from New York? He knew an awful lot about counterfeit money. Maybe the suitcase was his and he didn't want any money to get out in Pine Grove, so he grabbed Christine's twenty as soon as he saw it come through."

"Maybe it's Crabby Joe's operation," Meredith said, thoughtfully. "You know, someone can ship you a suitcase from anywhere in the world. You just have to go to the airport and pick it up. Maybe Crabby Joe is planning to distribute phony money all over the world."

"Or in New York," Nicki added. "He wants to open a restaurant in New York with Mr. Bence. Maybe they're into counterfeiting on the side."

"Hey, Nicki!" Joshua suddenly ran up, covered with sand. He pointed a grubby finger to a long cigarette boat that was cruising toward Coal Island. "Wook at that big boat!"

"I see it, Josh," Nicki said, shading her eyes to look. There was a smaller ski boat, too, cutting over toward the island. "There are lots of boats by the island today."

"How can they stand the smell?" Meredith asked. "I guess everybody likes to watch the baby pelicans."

"Can you take me over dere sometime?" Josh demanded. "In a boat?"

"Maybe sometime," Nicki said, as the smaller boat pulled away. "But not today. Now go on and play."

"You know, I was thinking," Scott said, looking over toward the restaurant where Dylan and Christine had gone.

"Maybe the bad guy could even be this Dylan kid. He works at the airport, right? Maybe he grabbed Nicki's suitcase instead of the suitcase with money, and then he just waited until she returned it. Maybe the only reason he's here is to find out what we know about the suitcase."

Nicki thought a moment. "Dylan *shouldn't* know anything about the money unless Christine tells him or he's involved somehow," she said. "But if he is involved, he doesn't know we know about the money unless Christine says something."

They all looked behind them where Christine and Dylan were talking out on Crabby Joe's patio. *For your sake, Christine, I hope you've learned to keep your mouth shut,* thought Nicki. *Or you could be getting yourself into more trouble.*

I think it's time for ice cream," Laura said, bringing Sarah and Josh back up to the group. "My treat. Let's go up to Crabby Joe's and get something cold."

"Sounds good," Nicki said, standing up. She grabbed a towel and wrapped it around her bathing suit. Fortunately, swimmers could come straight off the beach into Joe's ice cream parlor.

They trudged to Crabby Joe's, the hot sand stinging their feet. Laura ordered ice cream for everyone and they sat on Joe's picnic tables and looked across the water to Coal Island. Christine and Dylan were there, too, but Christine turned her head away and wouldn't even look in Nicki's direction.

Over at the marina, Nicki saw Wiley stretched out in his chair under his umbrella. As if he sensed her eyes on him, Wiley opened his eyes and caught Nicki's glance. She waved, but he turned his head aside.

"Mr. Wiley must not like us very much," Nicki said aloud. "He won't wave at me."

Laura frowned and looked over at the dock. "Why not? We didn't do anything to him *on purpose,* for heaven's sake. I know how to fix that."

Laura went back into the ice cream parlor and came out a few minutes later with a tall glass of iced tea. She stuck a straw into the drink and smiled at Nicki. "Let's go see Mr. Wiley," she said. "It wouldn't hurt, would it?"

Nicki grinned and followed Laura. Meredith, Kim, Scott, Josh and Sarah followed, too, but Christine merely watched her friends. She stayed at the picnic table with Dylan.

"Mr. Wiley," Laura called in her honeyed southern accent. "You looked so hot, Mr. Wiley. I brought you an iced tea."

Wiley opened his eyes and sat up straight. He looked confused for a moment, then he smiled and accepted Laura's peace offering. "That's awful kind of you, miss," he said. "It is a hot day."

"Are you out here every day?" Nicki asked.

"Nearly every day," Wiley answered, taking a sip of his drink. "I fish at night and rent boats during the day. I sleeps whenever I can." He grinned and a silver tooth flashed at Nicki. Despite his rough appearance, Nicki thought he was probably an honest man. Being a fisherman was hard work.

"Is that your boat, the *Puddleduck?*" Laura asked, pointing to the handsome sailboat tied to the end of the dock.

"Aye," Wiley nodded. "My pride and joy. I live on board. She's like a wife."

"She is beautiful," Kim offered.

Wiley smiled at them, and Nicki remembered something. "Mr. Wiley, do you know the boat that's anchored on the back side of Coal Island? We saw it yesterday when we were out rowing."

A strange look—was it worry or fear?—passed across Mr. Wiley's face, but then a smooth voice spared Mr. Wiley the trouble of answering.

"That's my boat," a man said. Nicki turned to see a

dark-haired man emerging from the cabin of the *Puddleduck*. He was polishing a piece of silver, probably some part of the boat. "The *Mary Celeste II*. She's not seaworthy right now, and I've anchored her there out of harm's way until I can afford to fix her."

"Oh," Nicki nodded.

"That's a strange name for a boat," Meredith said, eyeing the man steadily. "I'm surprised you'd choose that name."

The man laughed. "Marvin Novak may be a strange name for me, but it fits, so why change it?" he said. "It's bad luck to change the name of a boat, missy. So I left her the way I found her." He looked at Wiley. "Are these the girls who gave you the trouble yesterday?"

Wiley shielded his eyes from the sun. "Yeah. And no. It was all taken care of, you see." He winked at Laura. "There are no hard feelin's, I expect."

"No hard feelings," Laura echoed. "Well, we'd better get back to the beach. See you later, Mr. Wiley."

"Hey," Mr. Novak called, "You kids aren't planning to swim over there near the island, are you? I saw something kind of strange in the water yesterday near my boat. I'd stay away if I were you."

"What was it?" Meredith asked, unafraid. "A manatee? They wouldn't hurt you."

"Maybe it was a shark," Scott added. "Now that might hurt you."

"I don't know what it was," Mr. Novak shrugged, still wiping the silver object in his hand. "But I wouldn't take any chances if I were you."

Later that afternoon, as Nicki and Meredith sat on the beach watching the others swim, Nicki remembered: "Why did you ask Mr. Novak about the name of his boat, Meredith? What's so weird about the *Mary Celeste II?*"

"Would you name your kid Amelia Earhart?" Meredith asked. "Would you name your boat *Titanic Junior?*"

"Of course not," Nicki said, burrowing her feet into the sand.

"Well, what happened to the first *Mary Celeste* is an unsolved mystery," Meredith said. "I thought the name on the boat was familiar, so I looked it up. On December 5, 1872, a British cargo vessel sighted a ship floating in the North Atlantic. It was the *Mary Celeste,* a ship which had just left New York and was bound for Genoa. Aboard the ship were supposed to be the captain, his wife, their two-year-old daughter and a crew of seven."

"Supposed to be?" Nicki asked. "Were they there, or not?"

"The captain of the cargo ship had just dined aboard the *Mary Celeste* a few weeks earlier," Meredith went on. "So he was surprised to find the ship floating in the Atlantic, with *no one* on board."

"That's spooky," Nicki said. "But surely they could figure out what happened."

"Not really," Meredith answered. "The ship was only slightly damaged. Two of the cargo hatches had blown open, and about three feet of seawater had washed into the hold. A lifeboat was missing, and in the main cabin, a woman's clothes and a child's toys were scattered around. The ship's compass and navigational instruments were broken or missing. A blood-stained sword was discovered beneath one of the bunks."

"Wow!" Nicki felt a shiver run down her spine. "Now that's a mystery I'd like to solve. What happened on the *Mary Celeste?* Was it a mutiny? Pirates?"

"No one knows," Meredith answered. "The ship was carrying raw alcohol in barrels, and some have said that maybe the captain thought the ship was about to explode. Maybe the captain ordered everyone into the lifeboats until he was sure the boat wasn't going to explode, but somehow the rope broke or something, and they were set adrift in the sea. But no one really knows what happened, and I guess no one ever will."

Meredith shrugged. "You see why it would be really strange for anyone today to name their boat after the *Mary Celeste?* To a lot of superstitious fisherman and sailors, it would be like inviting trouble aboard."

Meredith's story frustrated Nicki. It wasn't fair that some things just didn't have an answer. She *knew* there had to be an answer, if only someone could find it.

It was just like the puzzle of the counterfeit cash. Someone had that suitcase, and someone knew that she and her friends knew about it. But who? She suddenly thought of someone who might be able to give her an answer.

D ylan!" Nicki called, as she and Meredith walked over to Dylan and Christine. "Got a minute? I'd like to ask you a question."

Dylan's eyes left Christine's and he winked at Nicki. "For you, I'll always have a minute," he said, and Nicki could see Christine's hand clench into a fist.

"Remember when I brought that purple suitcase back the other day?"

"Sure," Dylan answered, stretching his legs out. He leaned back against the table. "What about it?"

"Well, did someone come to pick it up? Maybe the lady who called about it?"

Dylan frowned. "It sat there for a long time, and by the time my shift was over, it was gone. I guess one of the other clerks gave it to the owner, or someone may have delivered it."

Nicki was disappointed. "So you didn't give it to anyone?"

Dylan shook his head. "Not me. Anything else you want to know?"

"No," Nicki said, turning away. "I was just curious."

"It was a good try," Meredith said as they walked back

to their beach towels. "We could have solved the mystery in a minute if Dylan had known who came by for the suitcase."

"Nothing is ever that easy," Nicki grumbled. "And we can't be sure Dylan's telling the truth. If he's involved in this at all, he could be lying."

"That's true," Meredith said. They sat on their towels and stared glumly out to sea. Joshua and Sarah came running up from the water, and Scott followed them. "Nicki, Scott's going to get a boat and take us to the bird beach," Sarah said, bubbling with excitement.

"Are you?" Nicki asked, looking up at Scott.

Scott grinned, and pulled his wallet out of his pocket. "Why not? Josh keeps saying he wants to see the pelicans, so I thought I'd rent a rowboat from the marina and take him over there. Want to come?"

"Sure." Nicki and Meredith got up and Nicki looked around. "Where's Laura and Kim?"

"They're down there talking to a lifeguard," Scott answered, jerking his thumb toward the water. "I don't think they want to paddle out to Coal Island."

"I guess not," Nicki said, pulling a tee shirt over her bathing suit. "Let's go. Anything's better than sitting here and broiling in the sun."

Nicki and Scott sat in the back and rowed together; Meredith, Josh and Sarah sat on the front bench and looked at the birds.

"Why can't we go swimming over here?" Nicki asked, looking at the beach surrounding the cove. "The place is deserted, and the water's almost flat. There won't be as many waves to knock you down, Josh."

Josh jumped up and rocked the boat violently. "Wait a minute," Meredith said, yanking on his waistband. "Let's park the boat first."

They rowed until the boat gently beached itself on the shore. The water was shallow, calm and quiet. From this point on the beach they could see Coal Island with its thousands of pelicans and just the tip of the anchored *Mary Celeste II*. A sailboat had just pulled alongside the *Mary Celeste II*, and was apparently examining the boat.

"Why do you suppose those people want to look at an old sailboat?" Nicki asked, as she stepped out into the water. Her foot sank in the mucky bottom. "Yuck," she moaned, trying not to think about her feet. "The bottom's gross."

Josh, however, didn't care. He pulled his inflatable swimming rings over his arms and plunged into the water. Sarah stayed in the boat, looking doubtful.

Nicki, Scott and Meredith pulled the boat securely up on to the beach and watched Joshua splash around in the water. "It's not deep, Nicki," he called, "the water's fine."

Nicki called to Sarah, "You can swim, too, Sarah."

Sarah sat in the boat, her chin in her cupped hands. "I don't like it," she said firmly. "The water's too dark."

Meredith shielded her eyes from the sun and looked over at the *Mary Celeste II*. "The other boat's gone," she said, "I guess people are just curious, so that's why they stop."

"It's really nice here," Nicki said, looking at the deserted beach. It was as if no human being had ever set foot there before. The waves washed ashore gently and rhythmically, and behind her Nicki could hear the hoot of a bird and the cricketing of insects. A horsefly buzzed near her leg and she waved it away.

Nicki spread out her towel and lay back on the sand. Directly overhead was nothing but blue sky and a few puffy clouds. The sun was setting in the trees behind her, and soon it would be time to go home for dinner. If their present mystery weren't so frustrating, it would have been a perfect day.

"Don't you wish summer would last forever?" she asked aloud.

"Naw," Scott mumbled. He was on his stomach, his head buried in his hands. "No football season."

"Brother," Nicki grumbled. She closed her eyes and relaxed, listening to the gentle lap of the waves. There was something almost hypnotic about it . . .

Suddenly, the quiet was pierced by a shrill scream. Nicki sprang up and looked at Sarah, who was standing in the boat and pointing toward the water. There was no sign of Joshua.

"Josh!" Nicki screamed, racing toward the water. She ran in and spun around in waist-deep water, feeling around. "Sarah! Where was Joshua swimming?"

"R-r-right there," Sarah sobbed, "But I was watching a frog on the other side of the boat and when I turned around, Josh was gone."

Meredith and Scott were in the water, too. "Don't panic," Meredith said, unable to keep her own voice from squeaking in fear. "Let's make a line and walk out, feeling for him. Come on, Nicki, we'll find him."

Nicki sobbed and looked around in disbelief. Surely this wasn't happening. She stood an arm's length from

Meredith and took a step on the mucky bottom. She beat the water with her hands, chopping in and out. "This isn't working," she yelled, and she dove in and tried to open her eyes underwater.

It was impossible to see anything. The water was dark brown and murky, and the muddy bottom was stirred by their frantic efforts to find Josh. Nicki came up for air and screamed, "I can't find him! Oh please, God, help us find him!"

She was about to go under again, but she heard a cry. Out in the water, about twenty feet in front of them, was Josh. His bright orange swim rings were bobbing on the surface of the water with his skinny arms through them, but Josh was screaming and bobbing up and under the water.

"Calm down, Josh," Meredith yelled, and Nicki and Scott swam toward him. "Don't panic!"

Scott reached Josh first, but Josh was so frightened he nearly pushed Scott underwater.

"Josh," Nicki said, reaching him, "calm down and put your arms around my neck. Don't choke me," she said, loosening his death grip, "just hang on so I can swim us back in. Okay?"

Josh's eyes were wide in fright, his nose was running and his mouth was open in a non-stop scream. His arms and legs were quivering, and he clung to Nicki as if she were his only hope.

Nicki and Scott swam back to shore. Nicki carried Josh out of the water, staggered to shore and collapsed on her towel, her lungs heaving. Scott and Meredith collapsed, too, in weak relief.

"It's my fault. I was supposed to be watching him," Nicki moaned, holding Josh close. "What if he had drowned?

What if he hadn't come up again? We would never have found him!"

"It's okay, Nicki, don't kill yourself," Meredith said, but her voice quavered. "I think God answered your prayer."

"What prayer?" Nicki said. "I was too scared to pray."

Nicki noticed that Josh was shivering and she gave him another hug. "We'd better get back to the beach," she said. "I need to make sure Josh is okay."

They picked up their towels and climbed into the rowboat, but Nicki's arms felt too weak to row. "Why don't you sit on the floor and I'll row for both of us," Scott offered.

"Good idea." Nicki sank to the floor of the boat and Josh crawled into her lap. She brushed wet hair out of his eyes and smiled at him. "What happened to you, Josh? Why were you out so far? You nearly scared me to death!"

Joshua looked at her steadily. "It was a monster, Nicki," he said solemnly. "I tried to swim away from it, but it kept coming. I went underwater and I couldn't come up. My foot got stuck in something."

"A monster?" Meredith asked. She looked at Sarah. "Did you see anything?"

"No," Sarah said. She was shaking, too. "All I saw was water."

"I'm not making it up, Nicki," Josh insisted. "It had wed eyes. Wong arms. It was weal."

"Red eyes? Long arms?" Nicki tried to think of a logical explanation, but couldn't find one. "Okay, Josh, if you say so. I believe you." She put her head on his. "I'm just glad you're okay."

Mr. Wiley just grunted when they returned the rowboat, but when Meredith told him that Josh had nearly drowned, he almost dropped his cigar.

"What were ya doin' swimmin' over there?" he asked gruffly, helping Josh out of the boat. "Didn't Marvin tell ya he saw somethin' weird over there yesterday?"

"I don't believe in monsters," Nicki said flatly, handing Mr. Wiley the oars. She stepped up onto the dock where Laura and Kim were waiting for them. "Especially ones with red eyes and long arms."

"You ask Marvin about it," Wiley said, nodding confidently. "He'll tell ya. He had a mate get killed by such a monster while divin' near Bermuda. Just ask him."

Nicki shook her head. There was no use in scaring Josh absolutely to death. He seemed to be fine, though, because in between the bursts of story he was telling Laura and Kim, he was strongly hinting that he'd like an ice cream cone.

Laura raised an eyebrow and caught Nicki's eye. "We nearly lost him," Nicki said simply. "Let him tell you all about it."

Kim and Laura led Sarah and Josh away toward the ice cream counter and Nicki, Meredith and Scott sat down at the picnic tables. Dylan and Christine were still there, deep in conversation, and Marvin Novak was coming out of Crabby Joe's restaurant.

"Let's ask him about the sea monster," Meredith said, her eyes glowing with curiosity.

Nicki didn't want to talk about it, but Meredith was already advancing toward Marvin Novak. She asked him a question, he nodded gravely, and together they came over to the table where Nicki and Scott were sitting.

"I did have a friend killed eight years ago in Bermuda," he said slowly, his dark eyes stirring with some deep emotion. "The authorities said it was a shark, but I knew better. It was a kraken."

"A what?" Scott asked.

"A kraken," Marvin repeated. "A giant sea squid. One that washed ashore in New Zealand once was nearly seventy-four feet long! If you hung it up beside a seven-story building, its head would be at the roof and its tentacles at the front door."

"That's incredible," Scott said, his mouth twisted in a wry smile.

"It's true," Marvin said. He propped his leg on the picnic bench and stared out at the water. "Sailors tell tales about krakens that wrapped their arms around ships and took them under. Their eyes are the size of dinner plates. Their arms can be as thick as tree trunks. Their bodies, if you can call it a body, are dark green or bright red."

"My brother says he saw something today over in the cove behind Coal Island," Nicki said, watching Marvin's face. "He said it had red eyes and long arms. It scared him so badly that he nearly drowned."

"You don't say." Marvin raised an eyebrow, then he

looked doubtful. "I don't think a sea creature of any real size would come up the intracoastal waterway. Water's too warm, too shallow and too busy." He shrugged. "Unless, of course, that's a baby kraken or something, and it just happens to like the quiet of the cove."

"You *believe* this?" Meredith asked.

"Young lady, I've learned never to doubt the wonders of the sea," Marvin Novak said solemnly. He put his foot down and straightened his cap. "If I were you, I wouldn't go swimming in the cove again. Come to think of it, I wouldn't go boating around there, either."

Marvin Novak walked away from them, his hands jingling the coins in his pockets as he whistled "Blow the Man Down." Nicki put her head down on the table. She felt very tired. "I hate it when things get complicated," she muttered.

"I know," Meredith said. "Now we've got two mysteries: counterfeit cash and the kraken of Coal Island." She let out a sarcastic laugh. "And both mysteries look pretty hopeless."

At six o'clock, Mr. Peterson walked down to the beach with an unusual proposition. Would the girls mind if their families joined them? Mr. and Mrs. Holland, Mrs. Cushman, Kurt Urban, Mrs. Dixon, the Parks and the Kelshaw clan were thinking that grilling hot dogs on the beach might be fun.

Nicki looked at her friends. "Sounds great," Laura said, twirling her hair. "I think everyone will go for it but Christine. She'll die if her parents come and catch her hanging out with a guy as old as Dylan."

"They'll make her wash her face, for sure," Nicki

laughed. "So why don't you go warn her, Sarah? Tell her that the families are on their way. That ought to get her moving."

Nicki was right. Within five minutes of Sarah's message, Dylan and Christine stood up and walked back down to the beach to the others. "Dylan has to go to work," Christine said softly, looking shyly down at the ground. "But thanks for coming, Dylan."

"No problem," he answered, smiling in his cocky way. He winked at Nicki. "See you guys around." Then he turned toward the parking lot and left.

"You timed that right," Kim said, smiling up at Christine. "But when are you going to tell him the truth about your age? You cannot hide the truth forever."

"I'm not worried about forever," Christine answered, snapping her gum. She pulled her mirror out of her bag and frowned at her reflection. "I've got to go up to Crabby Joe's restroom. Anyone else want to go?"

"I'll go with you," Nicki volunteered. She brushed sand off her legs. "I probably look a mess, too. Do you have a comb, Chris? I ought to fix my hair."

"I've got one," Christine said. They started walking toward Crabby Joe's and Christine began to babble about Dylan. He was so interesting, and knew everyone, and he had the best sense of humor! "Why when that lady with the dumb dog—what was his name? Oh yeah, Sykes—when she came by with that armload of packages, Dylan nearly lost it. He—"

"A lady with a dog named Sykes?" Nicki said, her memory ringing. Where had she heard that name?

"Yeah. A little Chihuahua. Anyway, she was carrying these packages to the post office, but she had the dog under one arm, and he tried to get at Dylan, and he couldn't, so he bit the lady in the armpit, and she dropped everything, and Dylan laughed his head off."

Nicki stopped walking and looked at Christine. She remembered now. The blonde lady at the airport had a Chihuahua named Sykes. What was *her* name? Nicki couldn't remember.

"You thought that was funny?" Nicki asked. "Why didn't you help her pick up her packages?"

Christine shrugged. "I never thought of it. Besides, that dumb dog was growling and barking and wouldn't let me near. So we just sat there and laughed."

Nicki sighed and opened the door to the restroom. Christine just wasn't herself.

When all the families arrived, Crabby Joe's slender stretch of beach looked like a block party. People were everywhere. Mr. Holland and Scott were playing frisbee with Tommy and Stephen Kelshaw. Mrs. Cushman, Mrs. Dixon, Mrs. Holland and Meredith were playing badminton. And all of the little kids were splashing in the shallows. Except Joshua. He sat on the sand, staring at the distant water of Coal Island Cove.

"What 'cha doin'?" Nicki sat down beside her little brother.

"Nuttin'," Josh answered. Then he whispered confidentially, "I'm watchin' in case the monster comes back."

"You really saw a monster?"

Joshua nodded. "Yeah. I weally did."

"Okay." Nicki put her arm around his skinny

shoulders. "I believe you, kid, and I'm going to try to solve this mystery for you."

"All wight," Josh said slowly, "but be careful, Nicki. Dat monster is weal."

13

That night Nicki dreamed she and Kim were back on the airplane coming from Atlanta. Mr. Bence from New York was there, watching everyone carefully and stroking his beard. Crabby Joe was the flight attendant, asking Nicki if she needed a pillow. But the pillow he offered wasn't white, it was orange, like Josh's inflatable swimming rings.

The blonde from across the aisle turned toward Nicki and whispered in a voice as rough as gravel: "Say I'm sixteen! Say it, or I'll sue this airline, kiddo! And if you hurt my dog, you're dead meat!"

Suddenly the voice of Marvin Novak came over the intercom: "We're sorry, ladies and gentlemen, but a kraken has just eaten the airport. You can see its red eyes glowing if you look out your windows."

Nicki looked out her window, and there was nothing but blackness and red, pulsating eyes glowing at her from below. But it wasn't the ground, it was water, and she was underwater and drowning. The red eyes were coming closer, and Sarah was screaming, and Meredith was shouting, "Don't drop those packages! Paging Marvin Novak! Don't drop those packages!"

Nicki woke up with a start and sat up in bed. She hugged her knees, reminding herself that it was only a dream. "A dream," she told herself, "a nightmare. And after a day like yesterday, no wonder you had a nightmare."

She thought about the dream and forced herself to laugh. It was funny, really. Why was Meredith paging Marvin Novak? That wasn't right—what was it she was trying to remember?

She looked at the clock. Six o'clock in the morning. Maybe it wasn't too early to call. Kim would know the answer.

"Hello?" A sleepy Kim answered the phone.

"Hi, Kim? Good morning. I need your help."

"Nicki?" The sleepiness was out of Kim's voice now. "What is wrong?"

"Nothing, really. I just need you to think. There's a piece of the puzzle that I can't remember and it's bothering me."

"What?"

"Okay." Nicki took a breath. "Remember the blonde lady across from us on the flight? The one with the Chihuahua?"

"Yeah," Kim was sounding sleepy again. "What about her?"

"Remember when they brought her dog out to the baggage claim area? They called her name, didn't they? What was her name?"

"Nicki, I do not remember," Kim sounded a little impatient. "Can't this wait until later?"

"No. Now, stop and think, Kim. Do that thing you can do with your voice, and see if you can remember her name."

Kim had an amazing ability to remember things she

had heard exactly word-for-word. She could even imitate voices perfectly.

"Okay." Kim took a deep breath. "The steward came out with his cart, and he said, 'Paging Marion Novak! Paging Marion Novak!' "

"That's it!" Nicki squealed. "Marion Novak! Do you think she's related to Marvin Novak?"

"Could be," Kim answered sleepily. "Good night, Nicki. See you in the morning."

Nicki lay down on her bed, but her mind swirled with questions. Who was Marion Novak? Was she related to Marvin Novak? Did she know anything about krakens? What was she doing mailing packages in Pine Grove? Did she know Kurt Urban? Did the purple suitcase full of money belong to her?

The only thing to do was take her suspicions to the police, Nicki realized. Someone had to tell the police, and Kurt Urban had withheld the only piece of evidence. So she'd turn in Kurt Urban's name. And she'd tell the police about the kraken and J. T. Bence and his handy counterfeit detector and Crabby Joe's business venture up in New York. And she'd tell them about the six hundred thousand dollars in a purple suitcase that she last saw with Dylan Ward.

"I should have done it in the first place," she muttered.

Nicki went to the police station alone. She didn't want to be persuaded by Laura, who would rant and rave at the mention of Kurt Urban's name, or Christine, who would freak out if Nicki brought up Dylan Ward. She also didn't want

Kim and Meredith involved anymore than they already were. Nicki knew this mystery wasn't something they could solve alone. Counterfeiting and krakens—that was just too much for a group of girls to handle.

She leaned her bike against Crabby Joe's restaurant building and looked over at the marina dock. Wiley was sleeping in his chair as usual, and Marvin was sitting on a picnic table sipping a drink. Crabby Joe and Mr. Bence were on the patio, looking out across the water. Crabby Joe pointed toward Coal Island.

Nicki's mouth fell open when she recognized someone else approaching. It was Dylan Ward, and Nicki ducked behind a corner of the building to watch. Dylan shook Crabby Joe's and Mr. Bence's hands. They talked, then the three of them went inside the restaurant. What was going on?

Nicki turned and walked quickly past the post office to the police station. She hesitated only a moment before swinging the door open.

A large ceiling fan overhead stirred the air, and a policewoman at the desk looked up at her. "Can I help you?" she asked.

Nicki felt her courage begin to waver. "I, uh, would like to ask a question," she said simply. Was she doing the right thing?

The policewoman smiled. "Shoot."

"Uh, if you found a counterfeit dollar bill, what should you do with it?"

The door opened behind Nicki, and the policewoman looked up to see who else had come in. She smiled at someone behind Nicki, and said pleasantly, "Be with you in a moment."

"Possession of counterfeit bank notes is a crime," the

policewoman said, looking back at Nicki. "The penalty is fifteen years in prison for producing, possessing or passing phony bills." She folded her hands. "So what's this all about, young lady? There have been recent reports of counterfeit money in cities around here, but none here in Pine Grove. Are you bringing me bad news?"

A dog barked behind her. "Hush!" a rough voice scolded the dog, and Nicki turned around. Marion Novak was sitting in a chair with Sykes.

"Um," Nicki turned back to the police officer, "it's kind of complicated. Why don't you help this other woman first?"

"Oh, don't mind me," Marion Novak said, puffing on a cigarette. "I just came in to get cool."

"If you want to smoke, you'll have to go outside," the policewoman said, frowning. "Smoking is not allowed in public buildings."

"So much for my rights," Marion Novak grumbled. She stood up with Sykes, and pushed the door open with her shoulder. "Have a lousy day," she called to the police officer as she left.

The policewoman rolled her eyes. "It takes all kinds." She looked back at Nicki. "Now what's this about, young lady?"

"It's, uh," Nicki paused and looked out the window. Marion Novak was walking down the boardwalk with her dog, and she paused to toss her head and talk to some guy sitting in a car in the parking lot. Who was she flirting with? Nicki stood on tiptoe and gasped: It was Kurt Urban. He was smiling at Marion Novak! He was getting out of the car, turning and coming this way! Were they working together? Were they the counterfeiters?

"Young lady, are you going to look out the window or talk to me?" the policewoman asked impatiently.

"Never mind," Nicki said, spinning around. Kurt Urban was right outside the door. How could she get out without being seen? "I'm working on a project," Nicki stammered, backing toward the door. "Research. A summer project. Never mind."

Nicki flattened herself against the back wall, and Kurt Urban came in and breezed right past her. Nicki caught the door before it closed, slipped through it and raced down the boardwalk toward her bicycle. If Marion Novak had tipped him off and he was looking for Nicki, he wasn't going to find her.

14

Nicki called a meeting of her friends that afternoon. They met in Laura's bedroom.

"I think I've figured the mystery out, and it's time to confront the criminal," she said evenly. "But I need your help to do this. We've never done anything like this before, and I'm a little scared."

"What are you talking about?" Laura said. "I hardly knew we were working on a mystery. Nobody's threatened your life or anything because you had that suitcase, have they?"

"No, but Joshua's life was threatened," Nicki said. "And that's enough."

"Tell us what you think," Meredith said. "And what evidence you have to support it."

"That's just it," Nicki cleared her throat. "I don't have any evidence. Just observations and a hunch."

"Tell us," Christine urged.

Nicki took a deep breath. "Okay. I think that Marion Novak was bringing in the counterfeit money in a purple suitcase. A woman could carry a purple suitcase and it wouldn't look strange, right? But she didn't want to carry it out. Too risky. So she had a partner pick it up for her."

"But you took it first," Kim added.

"Right," Nicki said. "But there was someone else at

the airport who hung around for a long time, gave up and then rushed back out when he heard that I had the suitcase full of money. It was your uncle, Laura. Kurt Urban."

Laura folded her arms. "That's ridiculous. I don't believe it."

"When Christine spent the phony twenty at Crabby Joe's, it was Kurt who kept the money from being given to the police," Nicki added.

"He only did that to save us," Laura said defensively. "We were the criminals in that case, Nicki. He did it to keep us out of trouble."

"Christine saw Marion Novak yesterday with packages to be mailed," Nicki said. "I think they are mailing the bundles of counterfeit cash out of Pine Grove, maybe all over the country. Today I went to the police and found out that cities all around here have had reports of counterfeit money, except Pine Grove. What does that tell you? The counterfeiters are headquartered here. They don't want fake money in this town — that would draw too much attention to them."

"You're crazy," Laura said hotly.

"What about the kraken?" Kim asked softly. "Does it fit into the picture?"

"Not really," Nicki said. "I think Marvin Novak just likes to scare kids, probably to keep them away from his precious boat. I think Josh was scared yesterday, but I don't believe there's a kraken in Coal Island Cove."

"Josh does have a vivid imagination," Kim said, smiling. "He told me yesterday about a blue and green sea serpent that lives in his closet."

Nicki nodded. "See what I mean? No, this has nothing to do with sea monsters and everything to do with counterfeit money. Marion Novak followed me into the police station today just to be nosy," Nicki said. "I tell you, she was following me to see what I would say. And then I saw her talk to Kurt Urban. He followed me into the police station, too, but I slipped out the door."

"Pretty slick," Meredith said, raising an eyebrow.

"You're all crazy," Laura said. She hopped off her bed. "And I'll prove it to you. I'm going to get my uncle right now and you can just tell him this stuff to his face, Nicki Holland. Then we'll see what you think!"

While they waited for Laura to reappear, Christine tugged on Nicki's sleeve. "Invite me over to spend the night, Nicki," she said. "Dylan wants me to go out with him tonight and I know my parents won't let me. But if I go to your house, he can pick me up and drop me off there, and my parents won't know. Okay?"

Nicki made a face. "You want me to cover for you so you can go out with Dylan Ward?"

"Yeah." Christine rolled over on Laura's bed and stuck a pillow under her head. "He's wonderful."

"If he's so wonderful, why is he a suspect in this counterfeiting mess?" Meredith asked. "I still don't know about him."

"I don't either," Nicki admitted. "I saw him this morning, too, down at Crabby Joe's. He and Joe were talking to Mr. Bence."

Christine crinkled her nose. "Why would he be there? He's supposed to be at work all day."

Nicki shrugged. "Maybe he lied to his boss, just like

you want me to lie to your parents. No way, Christine, I'm not covering for you. Not for this."

Christine sat up, her freckles blazing in fury. "I think you're just jealous, Nicki Holland."

Nicki laughed. "No way, José. I just don't trust the guy."

Kurt Urban's figure appeared in the doorway, and Laura pushed him into the room. "Have a seat, Uncle Kurt, and just listen to the crazy story my friends have dreamed up," Laura said, pushing Kurt toward a couch in her sitting room. "You won't believe it."

"I don't know about that," Kurt answered, sitting down and pulling a pillow onto his lap. "I know girls your age have great imaginations."

"A suitcase filled with six hundred thousand dollars is not a figment of my imagination," Nicki said simply. "Neither were you and Marion Novak this morning. I saw you talking together after Marion followed me into the police station."

Nicki quietly hoped that her theory was wrong. If she was right, what was she going to do? Make a citizen's arrest?

She told the entire story, from seeing J. T. Bence and Marion Novak on the plane to her adventures at the police station that morning. Kurt listened attentively, especially when his name was mentioned. "And that's why we think you are in league with Marion Novak, and possibly Crabby Joe, Dylan and Mr. Bence," Nicki said. "There's a counterfeiting ring operating out of Pine Grove."

Kurt Urban nodded respectfully when Nicki was done, and then he applauded. "That was wonderful," he said simply. "I love your attention to detail."

"So?" Meredith asked in the quiet that followed. "Is it true?"

Kurt Urban's smile vanished. "Close the door," he ordered, and Kim sprang from her seat to obey. "I'm about to tell you the real truth. Then I'm warning you girls to leave this mystery alone. The truth is more dangerous and serious than anything you could dream up."

15

"What do you know about the Secret Service?" Kurt asked.

"I know they protect the President," Nicki volunteered.

"We do," Kurt said, "but the U. S. Secret Service first set up shop in 1865 specifically to combat counterfeiting."

"*We?*" Laura asked. "You're with the Secret Service?"

"Yes," Kurt said. "But don't tell your mother. She worries too much about me as it is."

"Prove it," Meredith said. "Aren't you supposed to have a badge or something?"

Kurt pulled out his thin wallet and flipped it open. "Kurt Allan Urban is an agent of the United States Secret Service," Meredith read the enclosed badge.

"Wow!" Christine said, practically falling over Nicki's chair in her excitement. "A real secret agent!"

"Something like that," Kurt said, putting his badge back in his pocket. "And that's why I'm here. A counterfeiter has been distributing counterfeit money in the cities surrounding Pine Grove. I was sent down here because I have family in the area. I'm supposed to keep a low profile."

"A secret mission," Christine said.

"Yes," Kurt looked at each of them, and his eyes were serious. "You must not tell anyone, not even your parents,

93

why I'm here or what I'm doing. I'm only telling you because you've learned enough to get yourselves in real trouble."

"What do you mean, real trouble?" Nicki asked. "I was about to go to the police when I saw you this morning."

"These people are dangerous," Kurt answered. "People who mess with them have a way of disappearing. I'm sure they know you had their suitcase, Nicki, and they've probably been watching you. That's one reason I've been keeping an eye on you girls, too."

"You've been following us?" Nicki asked, breathless.

Kurt grinned. "How else do you think I managed to be in the restaurant that day when Crabby Joe found out you had passed a counterfeit note? I was there the entire time, waiting to see what would happen."

"But you didn't know I took the money," Christine said. "No one did."

"No, but after you told me about the suitcase, I figured the counterfeiters would want to know who had picked it up first, so I decided to stick around to keep an eye on you guys. That's why I was watching you this morning, Nicki. When you went to the police station, I wanted to see who would show up to check out what you were doing."

"Marion Novak did!" Nicki said. "She's got to be in on it. I figure it was her purple suitcase, see, and —"

"Just knowing is no good," Kurt interrupted. "We've got to have proof. We had reason to believe Marion Novak was the carrier for a counterfeiter, so I waited for her at the airport that day we all flew in. I had a search warrant for her luggage, but Marion left the airport that day without her suitcase. *You* took it home, Nicki."

"I'm so bummed," Nicki said. "You could have caught her right then if she brought the suitcase out."

Kurt put his hands on his knees. "We just lost that one round. But maybe it's best, because now we can find who's helping Marion. I don't think she's in this alone." He smiled at the girls. "Now it's my job to gather more evidence, so I want you girls just to have a nice, safe summer and leave the detective work to me from now on. Okay?"

Nicki was relieved to know Kurt Urban was going to handle things. She was even more relieved to know he wasn't a criminal.

"See there?" Laura exclaimed triumphantly. "I told you he wasn't a counterfeiter. Your theory was wrong, Nicki, admit it."

"She was close to the truth," Kurt added, rumpling Nicki's hair. "She's a pretty good little detective. I wouldn't mind having her for a partner."

"Thanks, but no thanks," Nicki said, feeling a little embarrassed and very grateful. She could have kissed him, except that he was *much* too old.

With the mystery safely out of their hands, Nicki and her friends decided to play putt-putt golf at Pirates' Pleasure down on the beach. Mr. Peterson picked each of them up after dinner and as they drove to the golf course, Meredith pulled out her notepad.

"I spent the afternoon at the library," she said, consulting her notes, "and I learned some fascinating things about money and counterfeiting."

"I thought we were going to let my Uncle Kurt take care of all that," Laura said. "Do we have to hear about it?"

"I'm interested," Nicki said. "Go ahead, Meredith."

Meredith grinned and looked down at her notes. "Okay. Our paper money is made at the Bureau of Engraving and Printing in Washington, D. C. Money is made out of a paper that cannot be totally destroyed. Even if you burn it, the ashes will still show that it was money." She laughed. "Once a farmer mailed in a cow's stomach, and the examiners at the bureau were able to verify that it contained several hundred dollars. They replaced the farmer's money."

"Wicked!" Christine laughed.

"Yeah. Actually, if you think about it," Meredith went on, "money doesn't tear when we crumple it, and the ink doesn't run if we wash it. It's made of strong stuff that comes from the Massachusetts papermaker, Crane and Company. The paper is shipped to Washington on an armored truck. Even having blank money paper in your possession is a federal crime."

"That's wild," Nicki said, shaking her head. "So what's this paper made of? Iron?"

"It's one-quarter linen and three-quarters cotton," Meredith reported, checking her notes, "with red and blue fibers added to the mix to make it hard to imitate. They use scraps from clothing manufacturers."

"How can counterfeiters get away with anything?" Kim asked. "It seems like it would be hard to make money."

"They're very clever," Meredith said. "Sometimes they even print tiny red and blue fibers on their paper. The best counterfeiters in history used the same method of printing that the Bureau uses, intaglio printing. They engrave steel plates, then the engraved plates apply the ink to the paper. The engraving is incredibly detailed work."

"I am curious about what the Secret Service does with

the fake money they find since it is against the law to possess it," Kim said. "Do they burn it?"

"Some of it," Meredith explained. "In their head-quarters, the Secret Service has two walls of filing cabinets where they keep four samples of every batch of counterfeit money ever seized. When a new counterfeit bill is detected, they can compare it with the others and find out if a new counterfeiter has set up shop, or if it came from one of the other sources. Every counterfeit bill has telltale charac-teristics, and all the bills from one counterfeiter will point back to him."

"That's amazing," Christine said. "So now that Kurt has that twenty dollar bill, he can compare it to the others in Washington and see which counterfeiter produced it, right?"

"Theoretically correct," Meredith nodded. "We'll have to ask him about that."

"I never knew it was so hard to make counterfeit money," Laura confessed. "I thought they just ran it through a copy machine or something."

"Those new color copiers are making it difficult for the Secret Service," Meredith said. "Because now anyone who has a color machine could be tempted to do just that. But the Bureau of Engraving and Printing is now printing money that contains a polyester filament imprinted with minuscule lettering running from the top of the bill to the bottom. The thread on a one hundred dollar bill, for instance, says, 'USA 100.' The thread won't be visible to copy machines. They have also put microscopic type around the portraits on bills."

Laura reached into her purse and pulled out a fifty dollar bill. Nicki rolled her eyes. Who but Laura would take fifty dollars to play putt-putt golf? But Laura was holding up the bill to the light.

"I can't see anything special on this bill," she said.

"You're not an expert," Meredith said, looking closely at the bill. She gave up after a minute. "I can't see anything either. Maybe we need that fancy counterfeit detector of Mr. Bence's."

"There's one thing I don't understand," Christine said. "If Marion Novak is a counterfeiter, where is she making the money? Does she have a printing press or something? Where is it?"

"Maybe she's using the color copier at the post office," Laura joked.

"She isn't making the money at all," Meredith pointed out. "The money came in the purple suitcase, remember? If Marion is involved in this, she's merely distributing it. Kurt said she was a carrier."

"Remember those packages you saw her carrying into the post office?" Nicki asked Christine. "She could have been mailing bundles of money to people all over the country."

"People pay in advance for bundles of counterfeit money," Meredith said. "It's a black market. People come to the counterfeiters and pay about three hundred and fifty dollars for a package of one thousand dollars in counterfeit cash. Then the buyers find other people to spend the money. Usually, the people in charge never get caught actually passing funny money. That would ruin everything for them."

"They just wait for dumb people like me to spend it," Christine grumbled. "And if we get caught, we're out of luck."

"The real people who get hurt are the ones who accept the counterfeit notes," Meredith said. "Hotel people rent rooms and get nothing. Restaurant people serve meals and don't get paid. People sell things and later have nothing to show for it but a lot of hassle with the police."

"And some people disappear because of it," Laura whispered, thinking of what Kurt had said. The girls fell silent, wondering who, why, where and how, but no one wanted to ask.

"Pirates' Pleasure, straight ahead," Mr. Peterson called into the back seat. "I hope you girls feel like golfing."

16

Golfing did help take Nicki's mind off their latest mystery. Besides, soon Kurt Urban would find the evidence he needed, and he'd bundle up Marion and whoever else was responsible and cart them off to jail. Life would get back to normal, and the girls could concentrate on summer fun. It had been exciting to brush up against a Secret Service investigation, but Nicki was glad it was over.

Pirates' Pleasure was a wonderful putt-putt course. There was an old pirates' ship in the middle of a lagoon, and four holes were actually played on the ship. Christine looked up at the ship's mast and rigging. "Cool," she said, and she started climbing up the ropes.

"Christine Kelshaw, you'd better get down before you break your neck," Laura called from the deck.

"It's really wild up here," Christine called. "I can see Crabby Joe's and the boat docks. I can even see Coal Island."

"Get down, now!" Nicki snapped. "Here comes the manager!"

The manager, red-faced and perspiring, was heading straight toward the girls, so Christine scrambled off the ropes and picked up her golf club.

"If you try that again," the manager shouted up at her, "I'll throw you out of here! Stay off the ropes! Can't you read the sign?"

"What sign?" Christine asked, looking around. Then she saw it: "NO CLIMBING ON ROPES."

"Oh." Christine rolled her eyes.

"Christine, what's gotten into you?" Meredith asked, steadying her putter and preparing to hit her ball. "Ever since you've started liking Dylan, you've been a real wild child."

Christine tossed her hair. "He has nothing to do with it. I'm just tired of people telling me what to do, that's all. I haven't done anything really wrong."

"No?" Nicki asked, trying not to sound harsh. "What do you call telling Dylan that you're sixteen? And asking me to cover for you so you could sneak out?"

"Okay, I've decided not to do that," Christine said. "But there's nothing wrong with Dylan thinking I'm older. Lots of girls are older, and they're free to do what they want."

"If you keep trying to sneak out, you may not ever be free," Laura said, teasingly. "Your parents will ground you for life."

"Let's just drop it, okay?" Christine said. She bent over to fill out her score card. "I'm thirsty. Let's hang this up and go over to Crabby Joe's for ice cream and a drink."

"Sounds good to me," Meredith said. "Let's hurry, though, 'cause it'll be dark soon." She collected their golf clubs and took them inside the office.

Kim added up her score. "My score was 95, the highest," she said. "Does that mean I won?"

Laura laughed. "The lowest score wins, Kimmie," she said. "And I got a 55. I think I won this one."

The sun was setting as the girls walked down the

boardwalk to Crabby Joe's. The dinner crowd had filled the restaurant, and a line of tourists waited outside for empty tables. Nicki and her friends walked down toward the water to the walk-up ice cream window. At least they wouldn't have to stand in line.

Each girl ordered her favorite ice cream, then they headed to the picnic tables to eat. "It's going to be a beautiful night," Christine sighed, watching the sun set. "Just look at that sky."

"I know what you're thinking," Laura teased her. "You wish Dylan were here."

"He sounded so disappointed when I told him I couldn't go out tonight," Christine went on. "But he took it okay, I guess. Maybe he can come out to the beach with us again next week or something."

"Maybe," Nicki answered, but her thoughts were elsewhere. Someone was moving over near the boat docks, but in the twilight she couldn't tell who it was. It was just a shadowy figure.

"Hey, you guys," Nicki interrupted their quiet thoughts. She nodded toward the boat docks. "Can you tell who that is down there?"

"I can't see anyone," Meredith said, squinting.

"Neither can I," Laura answered. "I thought you were going to let this mystery rest, Nicki. You promised my Uncle Kurt you'd stay out of his way."

"I'm not doing anything," Nicki protested. "All I did was ask a simple question."

They licked their ice cream cones in silence, then Christine asked, "Don't you wish Scott was here with you? This sunset is so romantic!"

Nicki sighed. "Are you guys almost done? We should probably walk back to Pirates' Pleasure or Mr. Peterson will wonder what happened to us. Give me your trash, and I'll dump it in the trash can."

Nicki gathered up their empty cups and napkins. The other girls slipped off the picnic table and began walking slowly up the boardwalk toward the miniature golf course. Nicki headed toward the trash can, but as soon as her friends were safely away, she doubled back toward the boat dock. She just had to know who was creeping around down there in the dark. It might just be a fisherman, but then again, it could be one of the counterfeiters.

She stuffed the trash into a nearby bin and walked out onto the dock. The figure was in front of her: "Oh, Mr. Wiley, it's you," Nicki sighed in relief. "Getting ready to go fishing?"

Wiley smiled, but his eyes darted from side to side in confusion. "Why, uh, yeah, I guess," he stammered, then suddenly Nicki felt a rough hand cover her mouth. She struggled, but someone dragged her off the dock and onto a boat.

"Hurry up and cast off while I get her into the cabin," the man behind her whispered gruffly. Nicki tried to place the voice, but it could have been any man on the waterway.

"You can't hurt her," Wiley said, the whites of his eyes glowing in the faint remaining light. "She's just a kid."

"She's a kid who went to the police," the man growled. "And she knows too much."

"You just can't snatch a kid," Wiley protested.

"Shut up," the man ordered, "or I'll make sure you go to prison along with the rest of us. Now cast off this boat!"

Wiley scrambled across the dock and threw a rope

onto the deck. Nicki felt the boat begin to drift. Whoever was holding her pulled her roughly inside the cabin, fumbled with something with his free hand, and the next thing Nicki knew was deep, throbbing pain. Then blackness.

17

Nicki's head hurt. "Ouch," she muttered, rubbing her head and opening her eyes. "That hurts."

She could smell sea air and hear and even *feel* the lap of the waves. She was in some kind of small boat, but how in the world did she get there?

The stars and a banana moon lit the sky just enough for Nicki to see water everywhere. Starshine glinted off the waves near her and the moon cast a long, silvery light over the waves in the distance. But that's all there was. Nicki was alone in the dark on the water.

Nicki bit her lip to keep from screaming. Maybe there was something in the boat she could use — a flare gun or a flashlight. But the old boat was nearly empty except for a faded life preserver that smelled of mildew, a rusty bucket and one rough oar. She could row her way home, but which way was home?

She squinted into the darkness, trying to make shapes appear in the velvety blackness. She wasn't in the intracoastal waterway because there were no buildings, no boats, no docks, nothing on either side of her. Nothing but water everywhere.

"I'm floating in the middle of the Gulf of Mexico in a dinky rowboat," Nicki said aloud. "Either that, or this is the wildest nightmare I've ever had."

What happened? She remembered going down to the

dock, seeing Wiley's flashing eyes, his nervousness, and feeling the rough grasp of the man who grabbed her from behind. One of the counterfeiters! Someone knew about her trip to the police — that was obvious because Marion Novak had followed her there — and someone thought she would turn them in. Scott and Kurt were right. Someone had been watching her to see if she would stay quiet.

"I guess this is their way of keeping me quiet for a while," Nicki said to the stars above her. "We were getting close to solving the mystery. They must be in a hurry to get out of town, and by keeping me out of the way, they can get rid of all the evidence."

She gulped. What was she going to do? She could float out here for days. They'd look for her at her friends' houses and at the boardwalk, but no one would know to search the Gulf.

Nicki knew she had to get a grip on her feelings. She had to control her fear.

The water splashed rhythmically against the side of the boat, and a cool evening wind blew Nicki's hair. Her teeth began to chatter. "Okay," she told herself, shifting her weight in the boat. It wasn't very sturdy and she hoped it didn't have a leak. Was that why someone kept a rusty bucket in the boat — to bail it out? "If I can just float until morning," she muttered, "then I can watch where the sun rises and row the boat east until I hit land. This is not difficult. I can do this."

She gritted her teeth to keep them from chattering and concentrated on the gentle lap of the waves. She wished she were home in her bed asleep, but home seemed a million miles away. And she couldn't go to sleep — she had to stay awake until morning.

Mr. Holland stood on the dock and thought about carnivals. That's what the scene reminded him of: red lights, bright white lights, men in strange outfits and Nicki—lost. He had taken her to a carnival when she was five, and she had wandered away from the crowd and been lost for an hour. He had found her, safe in the arms of a clown, and he had made her promise that she'd never wander away from him again. She had finally broken her promise.

Mrs. Holland was with the other girls on Crabby Joe's patio, asking for the hundredth time exactly what Nicki had said and done before they turned around and noticed she wasn't with them.

"It was nothing," Christine said, her eyes red. "She said she was going to throw our trash away. We walked up the boardwalk, and when we turned around, she was gone."

Even Meredith, usually calm in a crisis, was shaken. "Nothing unusual happened," she said. "We called her, and after a few minutes we checked the bathroom in Crabby Joe's, but she wasn't there. Kim and I waited here by the picnic tables while Laura and Christine ran to the limo, but she wasn't there, either. That's when Mr. Peterson called you and the police."

A police officer came up to the girls carrying a wire trash bin. "Look carefully, girls," he said, pointing to a stack of paper cups and a wad of napkins in the bin. "Is this the trash Nicki threw away?"

Meredith nodded. "I think so."

The officer looked grim. "This bin was down on the boat dock," he said. "Could she have walked down by the docks?"

Meredith shook her head. "I don't think so," she said.

"We were investigating a mystery, but we had given it up. She had no reason to go to the docks."

"Wait," Laura said, putting her hand on Meredith's arm. "Didn't Nicki ask something about the docks? Kim, do you remember what it was?"

Kim closed her eyes and thought. The next thing they heard was Nicki's voice: "Hey, you guys. Can you tell who that is down there?"

"Down where?" the police officer asked.

"The boat dock," Kim said in her own voice. "Nicki meant the boat dock, but we told her we did not see anything, so she dropped it."

"Besides, we checked the dock," Christine said. "We went down there ourselves and asked Mr. Wiley if he'd seen Nicki, and he said no. Marvin Novak was just pulling out on the *Puddleduck,* and he said he hadn't seen her, but he'd take a look around."

"Okay, girls," the police officer smiled and winked at them. "Level with me. Could this girl have skipped out to spend some time with her boyfriend? Or maybe she's unhappy at home and ran away."

"No way!" Christine blurted out. "Nicki wouldn't run away. And her boyfriend is Scott Spence, and he's probably at home. Alone. You can call him."

"I'll do that," the officer said, closing his notebook. "And Mrs. Holland, why don't you go inside and wait? The divers will be here soon, and you don't want to watch that. Go on inside."

Mrs. Holland looked at him as if she didn't understand what he meant, but she nodded and walked on into the restaurant. Meredith, Kim, Laura and Christine sat numbly on a picnic table, watching the grotesque scene in front of them. Out in the water, Marvin Novak was bringing in the *Puddleduck,* and he called a greeting to Wiley, who threw him a rope.

Meredith nodded toward Marvin. "Boy, I'll bet he's surprised to see all these people," she said. "Just an hour ago, everything was so *normal* here."

"I don't think I'll ever feel normal again," Laura whispered.

Kurt Urban walked up and put his arm around Laura's shoulders. "Laura, honey, your mother wants you to come home," he said gently. "She's worried."

"Do I have to?" Laura asked. "Nothing's going to happen to me, for heaven's sake. There are cops all over this place."

Kurt looked grim. "Tell me what happened." Meredith told the entire story again as Kurt's dark eyes carefully watched everything — the police officers, the divers, the men on the dock, Wiley, Marvin Novak, even the crowd of curious people from the restaurant, which included Crabby Joe and Mr. Bence.

"Where could she be?" Laura asked Kurt when Meredith had finished. "Do you know?"

"No," Kurt shook his head. "But I want you all to go home now. There's nothing you can do here, so go home and get some sleep. I'm going to have a look around."

18

Nicki thought the night would last forever, especially when sudden splashes jerked her awake. Once something thumped against the boat, and Nicki froze, certain that a shark had somehow sensed her fear. But when the sun began its warming rise in the east, Nicki grabbed the oar and began to paddle with all her might.

"That's east," she told herself, rowing on the left side and then on the right. "That's the way home."

When she thought she could row no longer, she saw green treetops in the distance. She kept rowing, and when her arms felt like they were about to fall off, she felt the bottom of the boat scrape a sandbar. Exhausted, she jumped out of the rowboat and walked slowly through the water to shore. The chill of the water actually felt good on her aching muscles.

The incoming surf nearly knocked her off her feet, but once she reached the shore, she crossed her legs and sat on the sand, her back to the water. She raised her face to the rising sun and cried.

"It's Nicki," Laura hung up the phone. "Uncle Kurt says Nicki walked ashore this morning up at Tarpon Heights. Can you believe it? They've called her parents and they're sending a police car from Pine Grove to pick her up. Uncle Kurt says we can meet her at the police station."

"Did you say she *walked* ashore?" Meredith asked, grabbing her notepad. "Where was she? What happened?"

"I don't know," Laura said, grabbing a doughnut from the table. "But let's go. Uncle Kurt will tell us the whole story."

"So that's what happened," Nicki told her story for the fifth time. She had already told the Tarpon Heights police, the Pine Grove police, Kurt Urban, her parents and now her friends. "And I really don't want to talk about it anymore. It was weird, like a bad dream."

"You're a lucky girl," the police chief said. "Now I'll bet you want to go home and change out of those salty clothes."

"Not really," Nicki said. "If we act quickly, we can catch the bad guys. I think they're trying to clear out of town already, and if they know I'm here with the police, they're going to dump the evidence and disappear. Right, Kurt?"

Kurt Urban nodded. "You've got the right idea. In fact, they may have already begun to cover their tracks. Wiley Stargills is missing."

"Mr. Wiley?" Nicki asked. "Why, he saw the man grab me last night! He must have known about the counterfeiting operation."

"Well, he's either hiding or he's been silenced," Kurt said gently. "I tried to question him last night, but the man simply vanished. We don't know where he is, but the *Puddleduck* is still at the dock."

"What about the *Puddleduck's* rowboat?" Nicki tapped her fingers on police chief's desk. "Why don't we let them think I'm still out to sea for a couple hours more? Then we could spread the word that Nicki Holland knows who left her in the Gulf and the cops are on their way. The bad guys will have to run to cover their tracks. In the meantime, you would stake out the places where they could be hiding their operation."

"You've got this all figured out, don't you?" Kurt said, a twinkle in his eye.

Nicki shrugged. "I'm pretty sure it was Marvin Novak who grabbed me last night," she said. "And his wife Marion has been mailing packages. But if Crabby Joe is involved, they'll run to him, too. Anyone who is involved should be flushed out. At least, I hope so."

Kurt nodded. "Okay. We won't tell anyone you're safe and sound until tonight. How's that? We'll set up stakeouts this afternoon and tonight we'll get the rumors flying. Then we'll settle back and see who lands in the net."

"Sounds great!" Nicki said. "Now what can we do?"

"No," Kurt said, pulling Nicki out of her chair. "You girls are going home. Stay in tonight and watch TV. Make popcorn. Tell stories. But you're off the case."

Nicki frowned, but she walked to the door with her friends. "I guess I should stay hidden," she said, "since I'm supposed to be out in the Gulf somewhere."

"That's right," Kurt answered. "Leave the stakeouts to us. Now get out of here."

Nicki and her friends slipped into the limo, and Nicki was glad it had darkened windows. She'd go home, take a bath, wash her hair and maybe take a nap. But she wasn't ready to give up on this mystery yet. Because of the counterfeiters, she had spent a terror-filled night in the dark, and she wanted to make sure they didn't get away.

The word of Nicki's kidnapping broke on the six o'clock news. "A local girl who was reported missing walked safely ashore at Tarpon Heights this morning," the newscaster read. "Nicki Holland, of Pine Grove, disappeared sometime last night near Crabby Joe's Fine Eating Establishment. Apparently the victim of a crime, Miss Holland spent the morning with police and gave details of her captors, their motivation and several other important pieces of information. Police expect to act on this information very shortly."

"That's great!" Christine squealed, pointing to the television in the Holland's den. "I'll bet the counterfeiters are running around right now, trying to figure out what to do."

"And the police have everything staked out," Laura added. "Uncle Kurt said they are watching Crabby Joe's, the hotel where Mr. Bence is staying, the Novak's home, the marina and the airport. They aren't going to go anywhere."

Nicki sat up, her eyes wide. "Those are the only places?" she asked. "They haven't staked out the most important place! Laura, can you call Mr. Peterson to take me somewhere?"

"No," Laura shook her head stubbornly. "You're exhausted, Nicki. You ought to stay put."

Nicki looked at Christine. "Please, Chris, this is really important. Will Tommy take me somewhere? Please?"

Christine tilted her head. "I think so," she said slowly, "but you have to let me come, too."

"Okay." Nicki jumped up and ran to her room. "Come

on, Chris, and borrow a bathing suit. We're going to board the *Mary Celeste II!*"

"I still can't believe we're doing this," Christine whispered as she and Nicki slipped through the twilight shadows along the side of the post office. Nicki put a finger across her lips and motioned for Christine to follow her. They padded quickly across the boardwalk in their bare feet and slipped into the shallow water at the edge of the intracoastal. Nicki quickly knelt down in the water.

"I know the police are watching Crabby Joe's and the marina," Nicki told Christine. "So we're going to have to swim pretty far. How long has it been since you went snorkeling?"

"Too long," Christine answered, pulling on her flippers. Nicki adjusted her mask and snorkel. She wasn't worried about Christine. All the Kelshaws were athletic, and swimming out to the *Mary Celeste II* would be no problem for either of them, as long as they weren't run over by a boat in the channel.

Nicki put on her mask and bit down on her snorkel. She took a few practice breaths, telling herself to be calm and breathe deeply. The sounds of the night faded and all she could hear was her own breathing. The world was a smaller place through her narrow diving mask, but she could get used to it. After last night, Nicki felt she could get used to anything.

"Okay," Nicki told Christine, taking her snorkel out of her mouth. "Stay beside me. I can't see you unless you're right next to me."

Christine nodded, and Nicki readjusted her snorkel. She looked down the waterway to make sure no boats were approaching, then she pushed off from the sandy bottom and kicked steadily across the channel toward Coal Island. She could see Christine beside her, swimming gracefully through the dark water.

As she swam, Nicki thought of Josh nearly drowning in these very waters, but she pushed those memories out of her mind. She thought instead of the previous night, when she had willed herself not to panic. That was what she had to do now.

In the gathering darkness, Nicki and Christine swam quietly toward the *Mary Celeste II*. The water was as black as ink around them, and Nicki tried not to think of the living things that might be passing by her in the warm water. Through her face mask she could see only the shrouded form of Christine, legs and flippers waving in the water ahead.

They swam to the stern of the boat, where a dim overhead light on deck threw shadows into the water. Nicki lifted her face mask. "Are you going to climb up, or shall I?"

Christine's mouth fell open and her eyes bugged. "Behind you!" she squealed. "Look!"

Nicki whirled around. Behind her something was rising out of the water—something big and dark and sinister, with arms like a giant sea serpent!

Was there a kraken in Coal Island Cove?

Nicki's eyes widened and Christine started to swim away. Nicki grabbed her shoulder. "Don't," she said, blowing water out of her snorkel. "Just stay here. Be still."

The creature did have shining red eyes and long arms, just as Joshua had said. It rose slowly, water dripping from its ghastly appendages, but then it stopped rising and began a slow descent. It disappeared, and a few bubbles broke the surface.

"We just saw Josh's kraken," Nicki said. "And I don't think it's real."

Christine bit her lip. "How do you know?" she whispered hoarsely. "It looked real enough to me."

"I don't think it's *alive*," Nicki said. "I think it's a fake, just like the money. It's only meant to scare people off."

"Are you sure?" Christine asked.

"Just a minute," Nicki answered. She lowered her mask, bit down on her snorkel and dove beneath the surface. She couldn't see anything, so she surfaced, blew out her snorkel and dove again. Then she saw it.

It hung beneath the surface of the water, a giant squid-like creature whose long tentacles rippled and undulated through the gentle currents of the water. But there was no sign of life. Nicki skirted the creature, and then she saw a long beam running from the creature's head to the bottom of the *Mary Celeste II*. As the boat rocked with the rhythms of the water, the creature rocked, too, up and down in a gentle motion.

Nicki swam directly over the "monster," her breaths sounding loud in her ears. She dove and put out a tentative finger to touch its head and an arm. *Aren't we clever*, she thought, *an old diving helmet with a red light inside and old swimming pool hoses for the "arms." Very scary.* She surfaced again and swam to Christine.

"Don't worry, it's a fake," Nicki told her, smiling. "What about the boat? Have you heard anything? Is anyone on board?"

"It's been quiet," Christine said. "The only light is that lantern way up on the mast."

"Okay, let's go," Nicki said. She pulled herself up on a long rickety ladder, threw her leg clumsily over the side and fell into the boat. If she weren't so nervous, she would have laughed.

She helped Christine aboard, then they turned to look at the boat. In front of them was the captain's cockpit, flanked by two benches. Past that was a small wooden door.

"Through there," Nicki pointed. "That's the cabin." Nicki gave the wooden door a gentle tug. It didn't open, so she gave it a hearty yank. "Open Sesame!" she cried, and the door opened. Nicki and Christine slipped through the opening and closed it behind them.

"Ohmigoodness!" Christine yelped when her eyes had adjusted to the dim light inside. Neat bundles of counterfeit money were spread on a table in the center of the cabin. "The money! We found it!"

"This means the police won't find what they're looking for," Nicki said, "unless we take some to them. They need evidence."

"Can't we just tell them about it?" Christine asked as Nicki slipped a counterfeit one hundred dollar bill out of a bundle on the table. "I don't ever want to even touch another counterfeit note. Plus, you're going to get it wet."

"Shhh —" Nicki whispered. "Listen!"

They could hear the drone of a motorboat in the distance, a drone that gradually got louder. "Someone's coming here!" Christine squealed. "What do we do? Jump overboard?"

"They'd see us," Nicki answered, looking around. She lifted a cushion on a nearby couch. There was a hinged storage box underneath. "There's storage on your side, too," Nicki said. "Get inside, quick!"

Christine crawled into the storage space on her side of the cabin. "There's something down here," she said, lifting out a small metal box. She quickly took it out and put it on the floor next to her. Then both girls crouched into the tiny spaces and pulled the heavy lids down.

The drone of the engine stopped and Nicki felt the boat sway as someone else boarded. It wasn't hard to figure out who it was because almost immediately Nicki heard the yap of a small dog: Sykes. She heard the cabin door open in protest, and in an instant Sykes was scratching the side of the box where Nicki lay hidden.

"Sykes, cut it out," a woman snapped. Nicki knew without looking that it was Marion Novak. The woman kicked something on the floor, yelled and then cursed. "Why'd he leave this out?" she grumbled. "That's just like my no-good brother, leaving our cash box out on the floor. Brains, that's what he has."

Nicki crouched quietly, hoping that Marion wouldn't open her box. What was the lady doing? Nicki could hear splashing sounds, then footsteps that led out of the cabin and back again. Marion was rummaging for something, then she was quiet. "Come on, Sykes, you can chase the rats later," Marion snapped. "We've got to get this cash box out of here."

Rats? Were there rats on board? In the storage boxes?

The dog's scratching stopped, something else splashed on the floor and even on the lid of Nicki's box, and then the footsteps retreated out of the cabin. The cabin door closed with a thud.

Nicki lifted the lid of her box. What was that smell? It wasn't the birds of Coal Island, it smelled more like a gas station. Like gasoline!

"Christine," Nicki whispered intensely. "Chris, she's going to burn the boat. We've got to get out of here!"

Christine's green eyes peered out of her box. "We can't leave now, she'll see us."

Nicki sprang out of her box and peered out the port-hole. She could see Marion and Sykes in a small fishing boat. Marion's boat was drifting, but she lit a match, smiled triumphantly and tossed it onto the deck of the *Mary Celeste II*.

"That's it! We're on fire!" Nicki flung the lid of Christine's box open and pulled her startled friend out of the box. Nicki knew the entire deck of the boat was probably already in flames and it wouldn't take long for the flames to reach the cabin. Nicki pushed on the cabin door, but it wouldn't budge.

"She's still sitting in the boat," Christine yelled in a panic. "She'll see us, Nicki!"

"Would you rather burn?" Nicki asked, looking

around. She picked up a broom and violently hit one of the portholes on the island side of the boat. The glass shattered but the porthole wasn't nearly big enough for them to squeeze through.

"Help me," Nicki said. "I can't budge this door!" Together the girls threw themselves against the cabin door, but it refused to open. The roar of fire surrounded them.

Think fast, think fast, Nicki told herself. *Sailboats have doorways and bathrooms and storage and portholes and—*

"The roof!" she yelled to Christine. "The skylight! Push it open!"

The girls stood on the wooden boxes and pushed against a skylight opening in the roof. The glass had been replaced by a warped piece of plywood, and it felt warm to Nicki's hands. She knew there was a good chance they'd be climbing into a raging inferno. But slowly the skylight cracked, and with another mighty shove, it opened.

Christine jumped up on Nicki's shoulders and scampered out, then she extended a hand down to Nicki, who scrambled up and out. The boat was a torch, but the flames were concentrated in the cockpit and around the cabin opening.

Nicki held her breath and motioned for Christine to jump out into the water, but she glanced over at Marion Novak. She was still in the boat, her face shriveled in anger and surprise.

"Jump, Chris!" Nicki screamed. "Toward the island! Now!"

They plunged off the side and into the water while the *Mary Celeste II* roared and crackled like a Roman candle. As Nicki and Christine swam and the pelicans on Coal Island flew uneasily above their nests, the *Mary Celeste II* lit up the sky and then, without a whimper, vanished beneath the waves.

Marion Novak wasn't going to give up. The *Mary Celeste II* was gone, along with the evidence the police needed, but she still circled Coal Island in her fishing boat, looking for Nicki and Christine.

"Come on out, girls. I know you're there," she cackled, reminding Nicki of the witch in *The Wizard of Oz.* "Let me give you a ride in to shore. I promise I won't press charges. You were trespassing, you know, on my boat."

Only the threat of Marion Novak could have compelled Nicki to swim into the murky waters off Coal Island. The pelicans, which seemed noisier and larger at night, didn't like the two girls who were panting and hiding in the shadows of the overhanging trees.

"Can't we swim for it?" Christine whispered, as Marion's boat passed them for the tenth time. "We'll be underwater."

"She can outrun us in that boat," Nicki pointed out. "And I don't think I want to be run over by a boat propeller."

"This is creepy here," Christine said, shivering. She smoothed the water with her hand and stifled a scream. "There's something in the water, Nicki! What if it's a snake?"

"Don't think about it," Nicki said. "We'll just have to wait a while, that's all. Marion can't stay out here all night. She'll probably take Marvin and the loot and head out of town."

"She can keep us out here long enough for us to get

eaten by sharks," Christine whimpered. "I just want to go home."

"Me, too," Nicki admitted. "But we can't think about that now. Just hang in there and someone will come along."

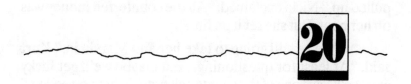

Nicki didn't think it was possible, but after about ten minutes they heard the sound of another boat approaching. Marion Novak stopped circling the island and headed off across the waterway to the marina. Nicki swam out from under the tree where she and Christine had been hiding.

A police boat was on the water, its red light flashing. Two uniformed policemen were on board, and someone else: Kurt Urban. "Kurt!" Nicki yelled, waving her hand over her head. Christine joined in. "We're over here!"

The boat's searchlight flashed across the water until it circled the girls. The boat slowly came toward them, and Kurt helped Nicki and Christine aboard.

"You know you girls are in big trouble, hanging around a bird sanctuary," Kurt said, a twinkle in his eye. "I think I ought to slap both of you in jail."

Nicki wrapped the towel he offered around her. "No thanks," she said. "But we have news for you!"

"We saw the fire," Kurt said, "and we realized we should have checked the Novak's boat. I knew you two were in trouble when Laura called me. She told us what you were doing."

"What a rat," Christine said, but her eyes were shining. She looked at one of the policemen. "Would you happen to have a cup of hot chocolate around here?"

"Marion Novak was here looking for us when you pulled up," Nicki explained. "All the counterfeit money was on her boat. But she set it on fire."

"We're still going to take her and Marvin in," Kurt said. "At least for questioning. And maybe we'll get lucky and she'll have one of the counterfeit notes in her possession."

"All she has with her now is real money," Christine sighed. "She took her cash box with her, didn't she, Nicki?"

Nicki nodded.

When the police boat arrived back at the dock, a large group of people had gathered. Crabby Joe and J. T. Bence were there, along with several police officers. Mr. and Mrs. Holland were there too, looking worried, and Meredith, Laura, Kim and Scott were on the dock. Even Dylan Ward was there, dressed in a uniform from Crabby Joe's Fine Eating Establishment.

Marion and Marvin Novak were in handcuffs. "We haven't done anything wrong. You have no evidence," Marion was saying. "You can't keep us in custody. By tomorrow night we'll be out of here. Wiley Stargills said my brother and I could sail to Jamaica in the *Puddleduck*, that's why I have the cashbox. It's our life savings."

"Come to think of it, we do have evidence," Nicki called loudly, feeling a little self-conscious in front of so many adults. She and Christine stepped out onto the dock. "Christine and I just came from the *Mary Celeste II* where you kept the counterfeit money. We had noticed boats circling Coal Island all the time, but we just thought people were looking at the pelicans. Then we remembered Marvin Novak's story about the kraken. He even made a kraken out of a diving bell and old swimming pool hoses. It's still down there, if anyone wants to see it."

"That's a bunch of nonsense," Marvin Novak said, jerking his arm away from a policeman. "She's just a kid with crazy stories."

"Yeah, like nobody'd believe you stuck me in a rowboat out in the Gulf," Nicki said. "But my friends saw you on the *Puddleduck* that night. It had to be you."

"You're nuts," Marvin retorted. "I'm a fisherman, and I fish at night like thousands of others. That's not evidence."

"Then how about this?" Nicki pulled the one hundred dollar counterfeit note from underneath the strap of her diver's mask. "We took it from the boat just before Marion came on board and set the whole thing on fire. The boat's underwater now, but I'll bet there's still plenty of evidence down there."

"I'll bet you're right," Kurt Urban said. He took the counterfeit note and held it up to a street light. "Chief, I think this is enough evidence to hold these two for tonight," he said, smiling at the police chief. "The Secret Service would be pleased if you'd do that for us. Tomorrow we can get a team of divers in the Cove to see what's left on board the *Mary Celeste II*."

"The New York City Police Department would also be grateful," said J. T. Bence, stepping forward. He flashed a shiny gold badge at the Pine Grove police chief. "We've been after these two for a long time, but not for counterfeiting." He glared at the Novaks. "People seem to disappear whenever they're around, and we want to find out why. I followed them down here, hoping for a break like this."

"Like Wiley Stargills?" Nicki said. "You don't think—"

Detective Bence smiled and shook his head. "Wiley Stargills is inside Crabby Joe's," he said. "I knew he'd be in danger so he's been under my protection since last night. He's willing to tell everything he knows to help get these two behind bars."

"There we have it," Kurt Urban said, clapping Nicki on the back. "We've got an eyewitness to several crimes, two pieces of counterfeit money and a girl who's awfully good with a rowboat. I think we have enough evidence to send Marion and Marvin away for a long, long time."

Mr. Holland scratched his head. "Joe, I don't see how you fit into all this," he said. "But if you're planning on engaging in undercover police work, your insurance premiums might go up."

Crabby Joe waved his hand and smiled modestly. "My brother is a New York City cop, and he asked me if I'd help Detective Bence," he said. "It was fun while it lasted, but I don't plan on doing it again any time soon."

Christine walked over to Dylan. "So you're working for Crabby Joe?" she asked. "You're not at the airport anymore?"

"No," Dylan said. "They fired me because I told my boss a little white lie. Can you believe it?"

"Oh," Christine said weakly. "That's too bad."

A young woman carrying a microphone stepped up out of the crowd and approached Nicki. "I'm with WTWT TV," she said abruptly. "Just look into the camera there and smile. And call your girlfriend over, too."

Nicki motioned for Christine, who ran over and wrapped herself tightly in her towel. "Do I look okay?" Christine whispered, smoothing her wet hair. "We're going to be on TV!"

The reporter interrupted. "Hello, I'm Jessica Walters and we're here with two girls who are heroes tonight," she said to the camera. "Nicki Holland and Christine Kelshaw swam out to a flaming boat and solved at least two crimes for the Pine Grove and New York City police departments. How old are you girls, anyway?"

She put the microphone in Nicki's face, and Nicki drew back.

"I'm thirteen," she said, looking at the microphone, "and Christine is — well, I'll let her tell you."

Christine looked sideways at Dylan, then took a deep breath. "I'm thirteen, too," she said into the microphone. "And what you said wasn't quite the truth. You see, the boat wasn't flaming until after we got there. There was a kraken in the water and Nicki swam over to it and said it was pool hoses, so we climbed up on the boat and tried to get into the cabin. Inside the cabin, you see, was a pile of money, but it wasn't the first time we had seen the counterfeit money . . . "

Christine babbled on and Nicki quietly stepped away from the microphone and into the crowd. She found Scott, who smiled down at her with his warm brown eyes.

"Are you really okay?" he asked. "You've been through a lot in the last two days."

"I'm fine," Nicki said, feeling a warm rush in her cheeks. She nodded in Christine's direction. "And Christine seems to be her old self again, doesn't she?"

Scott laughed. "I think she's learned to tell the truth, if that's what you mean. But I'll bet that TV reporter is wishing Christine wouldn't tell quite so *much!*"

They walked away from the dock as the crowd broke up. Kurt Urban and the police chief took Marion and Marvin Novak away to jail, and Wiley Stargills stepped out of the crowd and settled back in his chair next to his beloved *Puddleduck.*

As they walked away, Nicki could still hear Christine's excited voice: "And then we spent the twenty dollar note on ice cream, but Laura's Uncle Kurt knew we were in trouble, so he was right there, just like a secret agent. And Detective Bence was hot on the trail, too, and came out to help, but we knew something strange was going on at Coal Island. You see, it all started when Nicki picked up the wrong purple suitcase at the airport . . . "

* * * *

What's next for Nicki, Meredith, Kim, Laura and Christine?

The Case of the Haunting of Lowell Lanes

"Hurry," Laura urged Meredith. "This place is spooky when it's this quiet."

Meredith stood at the end of the lane, concentrating. Suddenly the few remaining lights flickered. A bright figure appeared from nowhere and seemed to float over the lanes until it hovered over lane thirteen.

"Ohmigoodness," Christine whispered. "This place really is haunted!"

Nicki and her friends thought it would be fun to help Meredith's uncle at Lowell Lanes for the summer. But then the lights went out and strange things began to happen. Is Lowell Lanes really haunted? Can Nicki and her friends solve the mystery before Mr. Lowell is driven out of business?

About the Author

Angie Hunt lives in Largo, Florida, with her husband Gary, their two children, and a Chinese pug named Ike. She and Gary have been serving in youth ministry for fourteen years. Her family lives on a canal where foxes, alligators, otters, ducks, pelicans and snakes regularly come to visit. She types out Nicki Holland novels while chewing her favorite food — extra-large red and purple bubble gum balls. To date, thank goodness, she only has one cavity.

Don't Miss Any of Nicki Holland's Exciting Adventures!

#1: The Case of the Mystery Mark
Strange things are happening at Pine Grove Middle School—vandalism, dog-napping, stolen papers and threatening notes. Is there a connection between the unusual new girl and the mysterious mark that keeps appearing whenever something goes wrong? Nicki and her best friends want to find out before something terrible happens to one of them!

#2: The Case of the Phantom Friend
Nicki and the girls have found a new friend in Lila Greaves. But someone has threatened Mrs. Greaves and now she could lose everything she loves. The girls have one clue that they hope will lead to something to save Mrs. Greaves—if only they can solve the mystery before it's too late!

#3: The Case of the Teenage Terminator
Christine's brother Tommy is in trouble, but he doesn't seem to realize it. Nicki, Meredith, Christine, Kim and Laura take on an investigation that pits them against a danger they've never faced before—one that could lead to a life-or-death struggle.

#4: The Case of the Terrified Track Star
Pine Grove's track star Jeremy Newkirk has always been afraid of dogs, but now somebody is using that information to scare him out of Saturday's important race. Without Jeremy, Pine Grove will never win! Following a trail of mysterious letters and threatening phone calls, Nicki and her friends are in their own

race against time to solve the mystery. Can the girls keep Jeremy's worst nightmare from coming true?

#5: The Case of the Counterfeit Cash

Nicki expected fun and sun in the summer before her eighth grade year—not mysterious strangers and counterfeit cash! Nicki, Meredith, Kim, Christine and Laura are warned to leave the mystery alone. But when Nicki is threatened, she has to solve the mystery to save her own life!

#6: The Case of the Haunting of Lowell Lanes

Nicki and her friends thought it would be fun to help Meredith's uncle at Lowell Lanes for the summer. But then the lights went out and strange things began to happen. Is Lowell Lanes really haunted? Can Nicki and her friends solve the mystery before Mr. Lowell is driven out of business?

Available at your local Christian bookstore.

Or have your parents call

Here's Life Publishers
1-800-950-4457

(Visa and Mastercard accepted.)